Epiphany

(A Journey)

A Novel by bdharrell

Printed in the United States of America

First printing 2018

ISBN: 978-1725686120

Dan Stevens was having a hard time with his faith and trying to manage the congregation at Magnolia's Community Church, when disaster struck. An arsonist set fire to the church in the middle of the night and burned it to the ground. When a church he was visiting in West Virginia is also razed, a shadow of suspicion falls on Pastor Stevens, cast by an overzealous sheriff. He soon finds himself on the run with an FBI sketch artist named Beasley, while other agents are on the trail of someone Pastor Dan thinks might have been involved.

Epiphany takes readers back to the southern Ohio town of Magnolia, as well as to the mountains in eastern West Virginia in a fast-paced novel some may find hard to put down. There are old friends, as well as some new friends who may find it hard to leave, once they've discovered the charm of Magnolia Ohio!

For all those who find themselves without hope. It's still out there for the finding.

Foreword

Some years ago, I attended a day-long "workshop" run by a preacher whose purpose was to sell his books. I had three takeaways from the workshop. The preacher had roots in southern Ohio; he was pre-occupied with money; and that preachers, or pastors, or priests, are prone to burn-out.

I can easily see the third – in fact, I have been acquainted with several priests and pastors over the years, and more than a couple of them have talked in private about the burn-out factor in their jobs.

Pastor Dan Stevens found out about the burn-out factor first-hand. Magnolia's Community Church is the largest church Dan has ever been head, or even sole pastor. Prior to his return to Magnolia to take the reins after the death of Pastor Kellough, Dan went from church to church, either as the "Youth Minister", or as Associate Pastor. Some of the other churches he had run were so small that he had to resort to turning a wrench to support his family.

Pastor Kellough was a hard act to follow. Add the pressures of a growing and active family, along with a niggling doubt or two about his own faith, and the next thing you know, Dan was ready to call it quits. There is where our story starts.

We're all on a voyage in this life. Sometimes the seas can get rough. What keeps us going is hope, and the occasional stranger to help put things in perspective.

bdharrell
September 2018

One

Reduced to Ashes

Dan Stevens woke up at three on a Thursday morning to the shrill sounds of two telephones and the wailing of sirens from the volunteer fire department at the north end of the street.

He knocked the handset off the bedside telephone attempting to answer his cell phone first. The bedside phone quit ringing. Before he could recover the handset, a voice from the listening end was practically screaming to him about something he could not quite comprehend.

Except for the word "Fire".

"Yeah..." Dan managed to mumble out. "Just a minute."

He reached his cell phone and flicked the icon on the screen to quiet the beast. Another voice said some of the words the voice on the land line said.

Again, the word "Fire" was mentioned.

The wailing sirens got closer. He managed to sit up on the side of his bed and put the receiver to the land line to his ear.

"Hey, this is Dan. What is it?"

"You'd better #### ##re quick. There's ## fire on South ####. Neighbors #### it's the church!"

Dan still had trouble processing what the caller just said. "Huh?" he mumbled.

"The church is on fire, Dan. You need to get there, quick!"

It finally registered with him. Steve Mulligan was on the other end of the line telling him that the Magnolia Community Church was on fire.

"Be right there," he mumbled.

"What is it?" Emily Stevens' voice floated over from the other side of the bed. She sounded more alert than he was. The racket obviously woke her up, too.

"Fire at the church," he said while springing up to see what he could put on to go outside.

Emily picked up his cell phone and addressed the other caller while he went into his closet to find a pair of pants and a shirt.

"That was Harold on your cell phone," Emily informed her husband while he dressed. "He called to tell us that the church was on fire."

The sound of the passing fire engine racing past the house headed toward the church confirmed that there was indeed a fire going on at three in the morning. Somewhere. "Please God, not the church," Dan prayed.

While he struggled to find a pair of shoes and some socks, she threw on a robe then went to check on the children. Frank, Frank the Dog was already pacing noisily in the upstairs hallway appearing as if he were an anxious mother worried about her children.

"It's okay, Frank," Dan heard Emily tell the family dog. He stopped on his way downstairs to reassure Emily and the dog before going out the door.

He raced out onto the sidewalk in front of the house. The sirens from the Volunteer Fire Department truck were winding down. Shafts of light from just down the street, along with a pillar of fire and smoke in the same general area confirmed Dan Stevens' worst fear.

Magnolia Community Church was on fire.

Dan's legs pumped faster than they had to for years as a shot of adrenaline rushed through his body. His emotions ranged from dread to fear and back again.

Doors on other houses opened and people came out to see what was happening. Some followed the pastor, some stayed put in the safety of their doorways.

Dan arrived to find a scene of organized confusion. Two women were busily tapping into the hydrant in front of the church while three men were unwinding the hose from the truck. He recognized them as some of the people living closest to the fire station. They were usually ready when an alarm came in to jump into their outfits and roll the truck to the scene of whatever emergency would happen to come up.

The women managed to uncap the hydrant and attach the hose running to the pump on the engine in less than a minute before turning the valve to tap into the water supply. In the matter of just a few more seconds, two hoses running from the truck started to fill with water. Two men, one on each hose, braced themselves against the expected kickback.

To Dan, the scene was surreal.

In front of him, engulfed in flames, was a building where he had practically lived and grown up. When he arrived to become pastor of the church just four years earlier, he did so with the joy of finally coming home.

The church was his refuge as a teenager, and a place of refuge to others, now that it was his turn to be pastor in charge of the church most people in Magnolia felt comfortable attending. When he arrived, it was the Baptist Church, led by an old, country preacher who never had an unkind word for anyone. Now it was just the Community Church due to Dan's influence and just plain stubbornness. Since there were several differences of opinion between Dan and other pastors of the Baptist faith, he took the church in his own direction. Ninety-five percent of the regulars stayed with him. The few dissenters were welcome into the building anyway. After about six months, most of them decided that they liked Dan's preaching more than they liked the old way of doing things and were welcomed back into the fold.

Dan felt a hand on his shoulder.

"You okay, buddy?"

Chief of Police Harold Richmond arrived. When Dan was a teenager tearing up the roads of Fuller County, Harold was his nemesis. Since Dan came back to Magnolia, Harold was one of Dan's best friends. There were also times when Harold was his muse.

"Yeah…" He answered, just now realizing that he was on the edge of hyperventilating.

"Some of the others are arriving and Roy's called in a truck from Prentiss to come and help," Harold continued. "Not much we can do except stay out of the way and pray."

Harold was right. He had a knack for being pragmatic and practical when the time came.

"Sure," Dan agreed.

The pastor stood in the middle of the church parking lot while people and equipment swirled around him as if he was a statue in the middle of a bizarre ballet. The flames and the smoke danced from the top of the building, mocking him – taking away a part of his life he could not easily replace. Harold guided him toward the periphery of the action. Both men eventually perched on the front fender of a nearby car to watch as the fire became more intense.

Two hours later, they were still there. Five in the morning found hints of dawn tugging at the horizon, while embers in what was once a pillar of the community glowed with a fiery light. At some point, Sheriff Roy Ball joined them.

Another army of townsfolk joined those who were on the periphery, offering coffee and hope to both firefighters and victims.

"I never thought of myself as being a victim," Dan observed as the first fingers of light pierced the darkness of that Wednesday morning.

"Maybe this isn't a tragedy as much as it could be an opportunity," Harold suggested. "A door has certainly been closed – so let's look for that open window."

Dan smiled, hoping that his friend was right. There might be opportunity salvaged from the wreckage before him, but it was difficult to imagine. Some of the faith which seemed to keep him going in the early years of his ministry appeared to be ebbing away. He likened the now smoldering remnants of the church to some of the same smoldering remnants of his soul. Some of the chores he took on when he accepted his position in his home town had become onerous. Petty quarrels and the overly-critical were Dan's bane. There were times when he felt he was less of a pastor and more of a referee.

He watched the fire department spray down the last of the embers and determined to find a new direction for him and his family. He would be finished with Magnolia, its people and its continuing drama to find peace elsewhere. His faith had been failing lately and he didn't care to continue. He was about to declare his intentions to his friend when his elder daughter sidled up to him.

"Momma told me to tell you that it's time to come home."

Gracie and Frank came to remind him that there was nothing he could do about his situation.

Dan Stevens looked up from the ground and saw a face. It was a new face. There was something familiar about it. Almost as soon as Dan's eyes met the stranger's, the other looked away then blended into the crowd.

Something wasn't right. A feeling came over him telling him that maybe the person belonging to that face had something to do with the tragedy laid out before him.

But now wasn't the time to investigate – to find out who belonged to that face in the crowd.

The heartbroken pastor gathered up what courage he had left to walk back home with his daughter and the family dog. Questions concerning what to do about the church would wait at least until after breakfast.

Two

Picking up the Pieces

Dan was overwhelmed by the outpouring of support in the week following the fire. When he wasn't taking another call offering to help, he worked with Sheriff Roy Ball, the State Fire Marshall, and the Bureau of Criminal Investigation. It didn't take long for the Fire Marshall and the BCI to determine that the fire was deliberately set.

Dan's reckless teenage years evading the Highway Patrol came to light when Harold Richmond (former Highway Patrol officer, now Magnolia's Chief of Police) innocently made a remark about those years with Jake from the BCI. As soon as the words came out of the policeman's mouth, Dan was subjected to intense questioning. Jake's questioning lasted the better part of two days at The Blue and the Gray. It was suspected that the investigator stretched out his inquest so that he could take advantage of the amenities of the bed and breakfast for as long as he could. Naturally, the delay kept Dan on "pins and needles" until the state investigator agreed to clear Dan of any wrongdoing.

Fuller County Sheriff Roy Ball called in the FBI as a back-up to the state's investigation after reading about a series of suspicious church fires in Pennsylvania and West Virginia.

Agent Rob Barada drove down from the Columbus office as a consultant. He surveyed the site, took notes, spoke with Dan, the church Elders and several other townspeople to come to the same conclusion. The fire at the Community Church was deliberately set by an unknown person or persons.

Barada's investigation cleared the pastor. He noted that Dan was more upset about losing the collection of books he inherited from Pastor Kellough than he was about losing the entire building.

"The house can be rebuilt," he told agent Barada. "Some of the wisdom contained in those books are lost forever."

Agent Barada also suspected a link in the Magnolia fire to the fires in West Virginia, Pennsylvania and Maryland. He forwarded his findings to the primary investigator of the other church fires.

When Dan mentioned the stranger at the fire, Agent Barada slowly nodded his head and said something about arsonists sticking around to watch the fires they set.

The only bright spot (for which, Dan was thankful), was that the church records had not been lost. Soon after celebrating the first anniversary of his arrival as pastor, Emily talked him into putting the information in "The Cloud" in the event of an emergency. Immediately after the fire, she resisted the urge to tell Dan "I told you so". He knew what she was thinking, and he was thankful that she didn't verbalize her thoughts.

*****

Immediately after the fire, the question of "… where do we hold services?" came up. The school board met in special session while the ashes of the church were still smoking and reluctantly offered worship space at the high school.

The school board's reluctance had to do with an incident several years earlier when the board approved leasing worship space to Pastor Winn Richards' congregation. A certain Miss Vera Mace felt that The Lord told her to stray from the assigned space one Sunday while the set-up crew worked. She used that time to liberally spread Chick Tracts around the school. Students discovered the tracts on Monday morning, not knowing whether they were a joke or if they would go into the bowels of Hell if they didn't repent right then and there. When the Superintendent, Claude Pepper PhD., found out about the tracts, he called pastor Richards on the carpet, tore up the agreement allowing the use of the building and told him never to darken the doors of the schools again.

Pastor Richards thumbed his nose at Dr. Pepper, pulled half a dozen trailers on a property three miles out of town, and started his own "Christian School". When the school held an auction to raise money, Steve Mulligan donated a dozen cases of a certain soft drink just to get a reaction from the petulant Pastor. As expected, there were a few choice words from the Man of God making the morning rounds at Zeke's café.

The pastor and the superintendent eventually came to an understanding and buried the hatchet. Pastor Richards still wasn't allowed to use school facilities, however.

Anyway, the Board of Education voted unanimously to allow Pastor Dan to use part of the high school for meetings on Sunday and Wednesday nights, provided there wasn't a basketball game scheduled. The summer basketball leagues graciously juggled their own schedules to accommodate the church.

Money was not a problem. There was still quite a bit of the seed money left by Katie Cole to get the rebuilding process started in earnest. Offers of help came in from all over the county and beyond. To Dan, the most touching donation came from his daughter Gracie on the day of the fire. Soon after he got back to the house and briefed the family on the situation, Gracie disappeared for a short time then appeared in the family room with her piggy bank. "It's all I have," she told her father. He used her offer as a teaching moment about "The Widow's Mite".

Offers of help came in from just about every corner of Fuller County. Gerald and Hank Windom at the lumberyard gave the church a blank check. "You're welcome to any materials you need to rebuild at what it costs me," Gerald told Dan over lunch the day after the fire. "And if we don't have it, we'll get it."

*****

Despite the outpouring of money and good will, Dan started to fall deeper into an abyss of despair about his faith. The Bible had become nothing more than words to him. He could no longer connect. He was burned out.

He went to the charred remains of the church the day after the State Fire Marshal released the scene, prior to the arrival of the clean-up crew. He was determined to see if anything could be salvaged. There was nothing left standing except for a woman in black; Miss Lizzie Elston from the bed and breakfast hovered near a section of the charred ruins. She was searching for something.

Dan watched her for a few minutes from a discreet distance, wondering what she might be seeking. She appeared to kick at some of the charred ruins with her feet before bending down to sweep portions with her hands. After repeating the same action several times, she came back up clutching what appeared to be a small object which she wiped and inspected before putting it in her pocket.

After several cycles repeating the same action, Dan's curiosity got the better of him. He approached the retired school teacher to ask her what she was doing.

"In case you have forgotten," she told him, "This is near where the front entrance of the church once stood. Just inside the door was the Wall of Honor. I'm seeing if I can recover the plaques on that wall before the trucks come to cart the charred remains away."

She showed him several of the small plaques she had already recovered. Each of them had engraved a name, a year of birth, the years of service and, if appropriate, the year the honoree died.

"These need to be saved," she told him. "These people need to be remembered."

Dan joined her in her task. They sifted through the rubble together for just over half an hour. Each found plaque was shared, noted and retained. Some Dan kept, some Lizzie kept.

"There were forty plaques on the wall," Lizzie told the pastor. "I can only account for thirty-eight between us. There are two missing."

Droplets of rain started coming down as she spoke. Dan looked at the sky to see that the droplets would soon become a steady shower. It was decided that the best thing for them to do would be to head for cover at the parsonage. They reached the house just after the skies opened-up – enough to get wet, but not soaked.

"I would think that both of you would have enough sense to get out of the rain," Emily declared when they stepped into the foyer. "Dan, go upstairs and get on some dry clothes. Miss Lizzie, come with me."

Emily led Miss Lizzy upstairs to the spare bedroom, grabbing a pair of towels from the linen closet on the way. While the spinster took off what she was wearing, Emily retrieved a dressing gown from her bedroom. While Lizzy dried off and put on the robe, she explained why she was out in the rain with Dan. When she was warm and dry in the gown, she gathered the plaques she collected then followed her hostess downstairs to the kitchen. Emily put Lizzie's wet clothes in the dryer while Lizzie arrayed the plaques she collected on a paper towel to see what she had.

Dan came downstairs to join the women, adding his collection of plaques to Lizzie's. He went to the sink to get a washcloth along with a can of Bon Ami.

"You said that between us we had thirty-eight plaques out of a total of forty," Dan pointed out when he returned to the kitchen table. "Looks about right."

They counted thirty-eight plaques just to make certain.

"So, we're still missing two," Lizzie said softly.

For the next several minutes, Lizzie, Dan and Emily cleaned the plaques enough to expose the names belonging to each of them. Lizzie wrote down each name, comparing them to a checklist she had in her head.

20

"You know that each of these has a story," she mentioned while they were taking stock. "The Honor Roll, as we call it, started soon after World War One at the old location."

"The Church and Grill, right?" Emily asked, referencing the former church building in downtown Magnolia which had been taken over and turned into a bar.

"Yes, that's where the original got started. The names on the original Honor Roll were painted directly onto a board and posted by the entrance of the church. When the second war started, names were added. Just the names, nothing else. When someone died in action, the date would be added. Mike McChesney who lived two doors down from this parsonage was the first. He died in North Africa. Others followed."

Lizzie scanned the name tags and produced the tag bearing Mike McChesney's name to show to Dan and Emily.

"When I came back home after college to teach, I became interested in finding out more about the names of the men on the wall," Lizzie continued. "By that time, the church had moved. The wall at the old place had been painted over and the only record we had of the names on the old wall was from my mother. She thought enough to copy the names just before Ed moved in and remodeled the place."

Dan was vaguely aware of some of the history of his church. He knew that attendance at the church had dwindled so much after the end of the Second World War that the building was sold and turned into a bar and grill. What was once a rough and tumble establishment softened over the years, becoming more family friendly by the time he was growing up.

"Not long after the new building went up, the elders decided to build a new Honor Roll," Lizzie continued. "My family donated the names and the money to make the wall a permanent fixture."

"I can understand why you were hunting for the plaques," Dan commented. "Your family probably had a lot invested in that wall."

"Indeed, yes," the retired teacher smiled. "More importantly, the community had a lot invested in that wall. Not in money, mind you, but in the memories of those who served and those who were left behind."

"You stated that there were forty memorials in the Honor Roll," Emily said. "We have thirty-eight. Do you know the names on the missing plaques?"

"I believe one of them belonged to Thomas Frost... Tommy," Lizzie answered. "He's still alive, living out in the western part of the county out by Jumpstart. He was a Marine in the Pacific Theater during World War Two. I used to go visit him with..."

"With who?" Dan asked after her voice trailed off.

She stared into space. Tears welled up in her eyes.

"Excuse us," Emily told her husband. She sensed that there was more than just a name involved... and that somehow, the name on the missing plaque belonged to someone Lizzie cared for.

Dan took the hint and left the kitchen, leaving the memorial plaques on the kitchen table to be dealt with later.

"The other missing plaque, the one you said Lizzie was getting all choked up about, belonged to Robert Clark."

Friday, a week after the fire, Dan was in Zeke's Café talking with Harold Richmond when the subject of the missing plaques came up.

"Bob was Lizzie's beau, after a fashion," Harold continued. "He served in the later fifties in Germany. When he came back, he got a job at the bank and started seeing Lizzie. Her parents never approved of the relationship. She was too high up on the social ladder to see someone who handled money for a living. As far as they were concerned, Bob Clark was dirt and they actually forbade her from seeing him."

"I suppose that they saw each other anyway," Dan surmised. "She said something about going to see Tommy Frost with someone. I assumed that she went with the other person whose plaque was missing."

"They had a clandestine relationship while her parents were still living," Harold revealed. "After her parents died, Bob and Lizzie continued to keep their relationship under wraps for a couple of reasons. She was afraid of her brother, Emmitt, finding out for one, and for another, the Superintendent of the school district at the time, Jonah Welles, wouldn't stand for it."

"Do you have any idea of why?" Dan asked.

"No one knows for sure, but it might have to do with Dr. Welles' service in the Second World War."

Harold drew Dan closer to avoid being overheard.

"The word is that Dr. Welles served in Europe – he claimed to have been part of the invasion on D-Day. He considered Bob Clark's service in Germany ten years after the war not enough to merit his inclusion on the wall. He would have had Lizzie fired on her way back up the aisle if she ever got married to him."

"I take it that the feud went on for quite a while," Dan said.

"Oh, yeah," Harold confirmed. "Part of the feud had to do with Dr. Welles not having a plaque on the wall. It was argued that Dr. Welles was only passing through Magnolia when he became Superintendent. He was never considered part of the community. Even though he was a member in good standing at Community Baptist, the Elders never considered that his name rated inclusion on the wall.

"Needless to say, that didn't sit too well with him, so, he insisted that if he wasn't going to make it on the wall, Bob Clark shouldn't have a plaque, either. So, Lizzie took down Bob Clark's plaque and held on to it until after Dr. Welles retired and moved to Florida back in 2010."

"So, Lizzie and Robert Clark saw each other anyway..."

"Sure did," Harold smiled. "They had a place between Peebles and Hillsboro close to the, uh... resort."

"Are you talking about the naturist retreat?"

Harold nodded his head. "They had their place since well before the naturists bought the property next door. Now, I've heard tell that they were both members in good standing at the retreat, too."

"You're kidding, right?" Dan chuckled. "Who else around here knew what they were up to?"

"It was pretty much an open secret to most of us. Hell, even Reverend Kellough knew."

Dan chuckled. "I would have never guessed it from her," he said.

"Nobody did," Harold smiled, "At least nobody who didn't need to know did. Everyone has a secret… at least everyone thinks that they do. Almost always, someone else is in on it."

"If someone else is in on something, then it really isn't a secret, is it?" Dan pointed out.

"Yes and no," Harold replied. "What do you know about the people who attend your church? You keep certain details in confidence as part of your job, now don't you?"

"Well played," Dan smiled.

"There are open secrets and there are secret secrets," the policeman continued. "Like when you were a kid, tearing up the roadways here in Fuller County being chased by a certain highway patrolman. You thought you were hot stuff and the patrol had no idea who you were. Let me tell you something. I could have busted your tail a hundred times over back in the day. I knew who you were, I knew where you lived, and I knew where you hid.

"Every lawman in the county knew where you hid," he concluded after a dramatic pause.

Harold let what he said soak in while the server came over to warm their coffee.

"The only reason you never got busted was due to John Kellough, and because you weren't doing no one any harm. If you were ever a danger to anyone, we'd have had you in "juvie" faster than you could say Jack Daniels!"

Dan and Harold enjoyed a hearty laugh. Dan liked having someone other than Emily to talk with without being judged. Part of his problem with faith was due to some of his flock's judging him behind his back. He had no idea what was being said, but he knew there was something because of the way certain people treated him.

Vera Mace, for example, would show up at the Community Church once in a blue moon to stir up trouble. Normally she was Winn Richards' problem. She would make her semi-annual appearances dressed exactly like she would have sixty years earlier, usually sporting some hideous hat. After sitting through services quiet and unassuming, she would make a point to spread her venom toward Dan.

"He sympathizes with those ho-mo-sexuals," she'd sneer.

"His wife breast feeds her child - and out in the open, too! It's not natural!" she exclaimed not long after Hope was born.

"That man's preaching is way too liberal for me," she huffed once.

"He's been ruined by that uppity wife of his," Vera complained.

"Those children of his are nothing but a bunch of little heathens!"

At that last complaint, Dan pulled Vera Mace aside and politely told her that if she couldn't say anything nice, she should say nothing at all. That last complaint took place eight weeks before the fire.

And while Dan Stevens watched his friend Harold Richmond leave Zeke's Café after discussing Lizzie Elston's secret lover, he groaned to see Vera Mace coming his way, staring him down.

"Well…" she harrumphed. "It looks like you finally got what the good Lord had coming to you! Now maybe the decent people in this town will finally have a church and a pastor without a liberal agenda for a change!"

"Good morning to you, too, Miss Mace," Dan said almost mockingly while a ripple of laughter circulated around the room.

Dan was not about to allow the woman to ruin his day

"What broom did you fly in on?" he thought. Providence held his tongue.

"Don't you good morning me," she declared loudly enough to be heard in every corner of the room. "There are those of us who've had enough of you, your family, and your liberal agenda! The sooner you're gone; the sooner this town can get back to normal again!"

She harrumphed one more time before turning around and marching right back out the front door. Out of the corner of his eye he spied the reason Vera turned and fled so quickly.

"Glenn told her a couple of months ago she was no longer welcome in here," Tricia Michaels told the pastor, her hand on his shoulder.

"Thanks, Tricia," Dan said, scooting over so she could sit with him.

"Not a problem, Dan," she responded. "You have enough on your plate without Miss contrary raining on your parade."

"You don't know the half of it."

"Yes, I do. Emily and I've been talking. She's worried about you, you know.

"I thought that was our little secret," Dan smiled.

"Sometimes you must have someone else to talk to, so you can maintain your sanity. You have Harold, Emily has me."

"She chose wisely."

"There's no doubt that your wife is a wise person," Tricia agreed. "After all, she chose you."

Dan enjoyed the company of the free-lance writer. She was everything Emily was – smart, witty and insightful. Like Emily, Tricia Michaels was almost universally liked in Magnolia – or for that matter, in Fuller County.

"Emmy tells me that you've been down, lately," Tricia continued. "Even before the fire, you seemed distracted."

The only other person aside from him to refer to his wife as Emmy was his father-in-law. Evidently, the two women were connected at a more personal level.

"We concluded that you needed some time off."

"I can't," Dan told her. "I have too many responsibilities, and Emmy and the kids..."

"And if you don't, you're headed straight for a heart attack. At the rate you're going, it's going to be sooner rather than later. I wasn't supposed to tell you, but Emmy and I have arranged for you to get away for a week, alone. You need that time for her sake as well as yours."

"What right do you have to interfere?" he thought.

Dan felt anger well up within him; at the same time, something told him that Tricia Michaels was right. He needed time – time to figure out his next step in life.

"As someone who loves you, I'm going to insist, Daniel Stevens."

"I suppose you're right," he surrendered with a sigh. "You say that you and Emily have been planning this?"

"Yes."

"Okay, then," he agreed. "If Emily says so, it's okay with me."

"I'll let her know," Tricia reassured him, patting him on the knee. "We still have a detail or two to hammer out, but we'll let you in on the plan in a couple of days."

Tricia got up from the table, paused to give Dan a quick peck on the cheek, and then returned to her regular booth. Dan looked around to see if anyone had witnessed what transpired. His eye caught Tricia's husband's eye. Glenn Michaels smiled, winked, and directed a "thumbs-up" toward the pastor.

"We both love you, Dan Stevens," Glenn seemed to say.

He felt the love from Tricia and Glenn, something he felt certain was between both couples. "But then again," he thought, "it's hard to keep a secret in a small town like this."

Four

Dan Goes on Leave

The idea of going on sabbatical grew on Dan as he walked back to the parsonage. At first it was a struggle. He realized that he needed time alone, but at the same time, he was overloaded with responsibilities. The notion went back and forth in his head without any clear resolve.

He deliberately went out of his way, so he could stop at Pearl's; the antique shop purchased and run by his father-in-law, Ken Griswold. Dan's sons, Jacob and Peter were there when he arrived, taking turns at the bubbler on one of the newer antiques. It was a soft-drink case – the bottles cooled by a flow of cold water. The cooled water supplied a bubbler on the side of the case which allowed everyone who wanted a free drink.

"I found this gem in a little town in West Virginia," Ken told his son-in-law about the cooler. "It sat around in someone's old garage for the better part of fifty years. We paid only fifty bucks for it and spent another two-hundred restoring it. I already have a collector willing to pay me a thousand cash, sight unseen."

"You said in West Virginia?" Dan asked while he inspected the machine.

"Just outside of Davis, on the way up to the ski resort. That's where Emmy..." Ken cut himself short.

"That's where Emmy what, Dad?"

Ken's face reddened just a bit. He suggested that the boys go outside for a while then pulled Dan aside over by the roll-top desk where he conducted most of his business.

"I may as well tell you, but you didn't hear it from me," he confided. "Emily and that reporter woman, Mrs. Michaels, are arranging a little vacation for you."

"I just talked with Patricia Michaels a few minutes ago," Dan assured him. "Actually, I came here to see what you thought of the idea."

"I suggested the where," Ken told him. "Emily told me a few months back that you were losing focus and asked for suggestions about what we should do. I told her you needed to get away. Away from here, the church, the family... everything."

If there was one thing Dan knew he could count on, it was that his father-in-law would be straightforward with him. The only difficulty Dan ever had with Ken Griswold was when Dan eloped with his daughter the morning after they met. The relationship between the men was strained for all of three days because of the elopement. After that, Ken and his wife were nothing less than doting, loving parents to Dan and Emily.

"So, I guess I'm expected to go alone," Dan surmised.

"You could take a good book or two... maybe your hiking boots, but for all intents and purposes, you will go alone. Your old roommate, Don Gooding, will be your host. He has a cabin tucked on a corner of his property, maybe five hundred feet from a hiking trail leading to Blackwater Falls. It should be nice and quiet up there."

Dan's face lit up. "How did you know about Don?"

"Emmy said something about him when I told her where I was going to get the cooler. I looked him up while I was there. Gooding seems like a good man."

Jacob, Peter, and another boy, Kevin Peel, drifted back into the store.

"Can we have some Ski?" Peter asked his father.

"May we have some Ski, and yes, you may," Dan corrected his son.

Each of the boys fished out a bottle of soft drink and took it outside. Dan insisted on paying for the drinks.

"Them sitting out there with the drinks will draw more people inside, hot as it is," Ken pointed out. "Besides, they're my grandsons. I get to spoil them any way I please!"

It wasn't long before Ken's prediction came true. Soon he was doing a land-office business selling soft drinks in between snippets of conversation about Dan's impending trip.

*****

"Dan Stevens, sometimes you are just impossible," Emily Stevens declared when Dan came walking through the door. "I've been planning a getaway for you since the morning of the fire. Daddy and Tricia Michaels called and told me that you know about my surprise."

"Harold and I were just talking about the impossibility of keeping a secret in a small town like this," he told his wife while giving her a kiss. "There are eyes and ears everywhere. You should have expected it."

As if on cue, the youngest Stevens daughter, Hope, came toddling into the room, followed closely by her older sister, Gracie. Hope lit up at the sight of her father, holding her arms up toward him silently asking him to pick her up. Of course, he did her bidding, much to her delight. Gracie and her companion, Frank, both wanted attention as well – something Dan found hard to refuse.

"Will you be okay with the kids when I'm gone?" Dan asked after the girls drifted off to play in the back yard with Frank.

"If I wasn't going to be okay, I wouldn't have made the plans to send you away."

Emily tried to give her husband the sternest look she could give him but ended up not being able to keep that look for long.

"Can we talk about this after lunch?" he asked.

"If I can get Hope down for her nap, sure," she said. "But I have a lot on my plate, this afternoon. I need to drive down to Portsmouth to do some research at the college library. Kevin's mom said she would stay here and look after things until I got back."

"In that case, I only have one question," Dan said. "When do I leave?"

He knew that once Emily had made plans, he would have a hard time dissuading her from changing them.

"Right after morning services Sunday," she told him. "I've worked the details out with the worship team for Sunday night, Wednesday and all of the following Sunday. Emma and Kevin will stay here to help with the kids. Mom and Dad said they'd help when they could. There's no need to worry about a thing."

"The woman has spoken," Dan thought.

"Thank you," he told her, holding her close.

*****

Packing for a trip for a man involves little more than making sure that there's plenty of clean underwear, shirts, socks and not much else. Emily insisted that Dan use a suitcase – for appearance sake if nothing else. He grudgingly complied with his wife's wishes. Packing with both of his daughters running in and out of the room proved to be a daunting task. Gracie had more questions than could have been answered by an Encyclopedia, while Hope kept wanting to be picked up.

Sunday morning services at the high school went smoothly enough. Sam Davis did as well as he could with the school's out of tune piano while the congregation did the best they could without their songbooks. Some of the lyrics got mangled, but the feeling was there. That was what was important. Dan mentioned his impending departure as part of the announcements.

"I know the worship team can handle things in my absence," he told his flock. "Just remember that God loves you and will take care of you."

"God loves you and will take care of you."

Dan had doubts about God taking care of him. His internal struggle was back. His faith was being tested. He knew he was being tested when the service was over, and he saw Vera Mace sitting in her car out in front of the parking lot. She gave him a mean look. He was sure that she would be back to cause trouble the following Sunday before he could get back. He had a word with the worship team about her.

"Vera Mace might be up to something," Dan told Steve Mulligan. "Keep a close eye on her, will you?"

Mulligan assured Dan that he would take care of things before the pastor went home to finish packing and having lunch before heading out.

Lunch consisted of ham sandwiches and light conversation. The Griswolds joined them along with Emma Windom, her son, Kevin Peel and Jaclyn Roberts. Jaclyn was Jacob's friend. She had just turned thirteen and was intent on making Jacob her first boyfriend. For his part, Jacob treated Jaclyn like one of the boys, ignoring her when he pleased. She stayed with him since early April, despite Jacob's lack of attention.

Goodbye was relatively short and sweet. Dan had changed into a T-shirt he'd gotten by donating blood for the Red Cross, and a pair of slacks. He and Emily tarried just a bit inside while everyone else gathered on the front porch ready to wave him along his way.

Two-fifteen with a five-hour drive ahead of him. Dan drove to the end of the block then turned east.

Thirty seconds after he was out of sight, a green Honda Civic drove up. Emily smiled. The guest had been expected. Gracie ran to greet their friend. Debbie Wallace had just come home from college.

Five

Catching up and Moving Forward

After a year of junior college, Debbie Wallace decided that she needed to get out of Magnolia to expand her horizons. She was eagerly accepted by several universities based on her perfect ACTs and the fact that she was co-Valedictorian of her high school class. She decided to attend Maryville College in Tennessee. They offered a full-ride scholarship including books, room, and board. She made up for the time she lost because of her unexpected pregnancy and subsequent miscarriage by staying on campus the previous summer instead of heading home. Except for a couple of short Christmas visits, she hadn't been back in Magnolia for nearly two years.

As far as Gracie was concerned, Debbie was a sight for sore eyes. The pair spent a good ten minutes on the front porch with Gracie rattling off every bit of news which was fit to tell the young woman. Gracie had to tell Debbie all about her new sister. Emily kept close, guiding her daughter's words so as not to upset the collegian.

"I hope she hasn't upset you," Emily told their new guest after they went back inside.

"Well, I am still a little melancholy about what happened and what could have been," she told her host. "But I'm okay. When I'm down, I tell myself that that's all behind me now. I have a wonderful life ahead."

A quick hug was exchanged before they turned to go inside.

"Emma Windom's here," Emily told the younger woman, hoping to avoid any possible conflict.

Emma's grown step-son Hank was the father of the child Debbie could have had.

"It's okay," Debbie assured her host. "I was going to Windom's to see Hank once I'd finished saying hi, here. Emma and I are okay with it."

The subject was dropped before they went on into the house.

Emma and Debbie greeted each other warmly when she came into the kitchen. Emily was a bit puzzled at the exchange, since she presumed that there was still animosity between Debbie and the Windom family because of the awkward situation involving Debbie's unexpected pregnancy and her subsequent miscarriage.

Emily, her mother, Debbie, and Emma Windom spent an hour chatting about a variety of subjects before Emma excused herself to go home.

"I knew that you and Hank buried the hatchet when you left town to go to college," Emily stated once Emma left. "But I also thought that you hadn't been talking to him."

"We weren't talking. For a long time, I was angry at him because of what happened," Debbie revealed. "Part of the reason is that people treated me differently after the miscarriage. I quit working at Mulligans much sooner than I would have otherwise. You were one of very few people who seemed to understand."

Emily accepted the compliment.

"I take it that something's changed?" she asked.

"The situation changed," Debbie told Emily. "I had a long talk with Jaybo Hatfield at the Mental Health Center. He pointed out a few things I hadn't thought of and suggested that I start a conversation with Hank. We talked. Hank and I both grew since I went off to school. I've forgiven him. More importantly, I've forgiven myself for being so foolish.

"Besides," Debbie winked, "Now that he's matured, and I've gotten to know him better, I... sort of like him."

Emily smiled and gave her friend a hug before she had to leave.

"Mom, Dad and my little brother are expecting me at the house," Debbie excused herself. "And I do want to talk with Hank before I head back to Mom's. See you later!"

Debbie had a quick word with Gracie before driving off.

Emily and her mother stayed in the kitchen for some quiet conversation about their unexpected guest.

"She might have stayed here had it not been for the shaming," Emily concluded. "The summer before she left, she hardly ever left the house except to come over here."

"It's a shame. She seems like such a nice girl."

"Oh, she is," Emily assured her mother. "It's just that... well, you know about how things can be in a small town. Debbie's friend and co-valedictorian, Cale, for instance, left to go to Cleveland just after Christmas last year because of all the talk about his being gay. It didn't matter to his adoptive parents, and it didn't matter to his biological parents, either. It's just that some people wouldn't let go."

"I know how rumors can be," her mother commiserated. "I've heard some awful things said about Dan recently."

"What's being said?" Debbie asked.

"Nothing but idle gossip, dear."

"Mother, please," Emily pleaded. "Dan has enough on his plate without dredging up idle gossip. That's why we sent him away. Whatever it is that's bothering Dan will likely go away once he comes back from his trip."

Emily was hopeful, but not much. She had an inkling of the extent of Dan's internal struggle. Since the fire, he appeared to her even more troubled than he was in the months before the fire. There was a change coming to Pastor Dan Stevens, a change which would alter their relationship. She retreated into her husband's study not knowing if that change would be for better or for worse.

Dan felt guilty about leaving his wife and the elders in charge for a week while he spent time alone. He felt as if he had betrayed the trust of his congregation – maybe somehow leading them astray in their time of need. The burned-out shell of the church stood the test of time for as long as he could remember. It came down on his watch. Even though agent Barada of the FBI told him that he shouldn't be worried about being a suspect in the conflagration, he was still worried.

The worry gnawed at him.

Jackson, Wellston, Athens, Belpre, Parkersburg. Between Parkersburg and Clarksburg, he navigated the roller-coaster of hills, starting to take delight in the drive itself. It had been a while since he'd been out, heeding the call of the open road. For a while, he wished he was driving something else. Tricia Michaels' Mustang would be nice. Top down with Emily by his side would be even better.

A glance in the rear-view mirror confirmed that he was in Emily's Malibu, just slightly over the speed limit and under the careful eye of the West Virginia State Police.

"It was good while it lasted," he sighed.

He stopped at the top of the hill in Bridgeport to determine which way he wanted to drive out to Davis. After pondering for ten minutes, he decided that driving down the Interstate for a few miles until he caught

Route 33 was a safer alternative to attempting the switchbacks along Route 50.

He had softened with age.

Someone in a Corvette zoomed past him doing at least 90 while on the Interstate. The same car was pulled over to the side of the road just before his exit.

Dan thought about pulling to the side to take a picture to send to Harold back in Magnolia. He knew Harold would appreciate seeing that at least one Highway Patrolman was on the job and able to catch his quarry. A smile appeared on Dan's face while he recalled playing cat and mouse with Harold Richmond out on the roads of Fuller County back in the day.

His mind wandered back to Emily. She appeared to have caught the faith he once had, and now, she might feel betrayed. Fear started to cloud his mind again. He imagined that she appeared to be almost anxious to get him on the road to West Virginia. Was this part of the post-partum blues which seemed to hit her especially hard after the birth of their youngest daughter, Hope?

Buckhannon slipped by, followed by Elkins. Hills became mountains. The four-lane finally petered out. The Malibu started to show signs that it wasn't quite as happy as it was on the relatively flat landscape back in Ohio.

At Harmon, he headed north toward Davis. The road twisted and turned for a while before straightening out in the broad Canaan Valley. He drove at a quick clip so that he could get to town and perhaps catch services at the church where his friend and host, Pastor Donald Gooding preached.

Pastor Gooding's congregation was on their way out of the white frame church when Dan arrived. Donald Gooding was a lean man with a ready smile. His hair seemed to be a crashing blonde wave on his head. Dan knew that his host had been fighting with a naturally wavy head of hair for most of his life. He also knew that his friend was due for a visit to the barber.

"Dan!" the pastor exclaimed when he spotted his visitor. "I see you've made it!"

He said a few words to the man he was talking to while Dan approached.

"Dan, I'd like you to meet George Pinkerman; he's the sheriff in these parts."

Sheriff Pinkerman was stocky, relatively short with the bearing of a Marine Drill Sergeant at boot camp, complete with a crew cut.

"Pastor Donald was telling me about your church over in Ohio," the sheriff said while shaking Dan's hand. "Sorry to hear about your loss."

"Buildings can be rebuilt, but some of what was lost was irreplaceable," Dan explained. "My office had records going back nearly sixty years. Insurance will pay for much of what was lost, but there were books in my office which can never be recovered."

"Jennifer and I took the precaution of filing a duplicate set of records once we heard about what happened to Dan's church in Magnolia," Pastor Gooding remarked. "Emily, Dan's wife, suggested that we do it when she was setting up Dan's visit."

"Hope you never have to use them," Sheriff Pinkerman smiled.

The sheriff excused himself. Dan and Pastor Donald met a few other people who had lingered before going back into the church to meet Donald's wife, Jennifer, prior to locking up for the night. Dan and the local pastor talked shop for a while before taking the drive up to Donald and Jennifer's home near the head of Canaan Valley.

"The guest cabin is a quarter of a mile on up the driveway from the house," Pastor Donald instructed when they arrived at his house. "You'll have a hot tub and a whole lot of privacy. If you want, there's a path leading up to the trail between the resort and town. There are a couple of vistas no more than two miles either direction of where the path meets the trail. I left a map on the kitchen counter next to the sink for your convenience. Just keep an eye out for bears and snakes. For the most part, they'll leave you alone, but you can never be too careful."

Dan thanked his host then drove on up to the guest cabin, hoping that there was food in the refrigerator. He didn't need to worry. The larder contained a wide variety of comestibles. Dan prepared a Reuben sandwich – a guilty pleasure left over from his days in Bible college. Dan and Donald would occasionally sneak off to a certain restaurant off campus which served what both thought was the best Reuben they'd ever tasted. Both had eyes for the waitress – a pretty, young woman working her way through junior college, not knowing yet her life's calling. It was during Dan and Donald's second year at the Bible college that Donald asked the waitress to be his wife. "It's just for the sandwiches, you see," Donald told his roommate when he revealed the engagement.

Dan lingered over his sandwich and a handful of salt and pepper potato chips while looking over the map provided by his host. He thought briefly about taking a flashlight and venturing out along the path from the cabin to hook up with the trail. Instead, he decided to take advantage of the hot tub. Before going in, he took a quick shower and arranged for music through his cell phone and a wireless speaker. After setting up on the back porch, he thought he'd heard something.

"Donald or Jennifer sneaking up the driveway, I imagine," he said to himself.

He heard only one set of footsteps and concluded that is was probably Jennifer. She sought him out from time to time for advice and insight. Dan wished that he had some to give her. He thought about going around the cabin to see if it was Jennifer, and to invite her to join him in the hot tub.

But it would be a betrayal to one of his best friends, and to Emily.

He thought back to a tryst he had had with Jennifer just a few months before she and Donald announced they were getting engaged. The thought of her body next to his again was enticing, even after a twenty-two-year gap.

He shook it off.

They were both married, now. Even if they kept the rendezvous he was daydreaming about, they were both responsible adults with too many ties to other relationships to justify the risk of being caught.

In that moment, he thought he heard someone heading back down the driveway on foot. Then again, his mind might have been playing tricks on him. Night sounds in rural West Virginia were quite different than night sounds in a small town in Ohio.

He decided to forego listening to the music coming from his phone to instead listen to the sounds of a peaceful night.

Seven

Unsettling Encounters

There was something missing or something added. Dan couldn't determine exactly what was going on when he woke up at three in the morning. He reached over just to touch Emily for reassurance before he realized that he was alone in an unfamiliar place.

He turned over, thinking that if he positioned himself just a little differently he might fall right back asleep.

Three-fifteen.

He shouldn't have turned his cell phone over to see the time.

Too late.

He was anxious about something.

Nothing.

He got up to use the bathroom, barely recalling where he could find the bathroom. The sound of his urine hitting the water in the toilet reassured him.

He was ready. He could go back to sleep.

Three-thirty-three.

Damn.

He threw the covers off, hoping to dissipate the warmth of his body into the room around him.

Dan was either too hot or too cold for another half an hour.

At four-twelve he finally surrendered. Sleep eluded him.

Why?

He had no schedule, no agenda for the day. Breakfast followed by a hike in the surrounding woods followed by…

There was no agenda.

He wandered to the front door of the cabin, hesitating ever so briefly before opening the door and stepping outside. A cool mist enveloped him. He breathed in deeply then became fully awake.

The cacophony of night noises which lulled him asleep just a few hours before, abated as if in anticipation of the cool, quiet dawn. Those noises were replaced by the rhythmic chirping of birds in the surrounding forest, abetted by the quiet rush of forest animals going about their usual morning routines.

"God's still alive."

The stillness made him hopeful. He stood on the cabin porch taking in what the morning revealed. After several deep breaths, he went inside to put on clothes and a pair of running shoes.

He waited until there was enough light to allow him to run unhindered along a path leading down to the main road where he could do an easy five miles before traffic became an issue. On the return trip, he was paced for half a mile by a sheriff's deputy who was friendly enough to offer words of encouragement when he passed.

"God's still alive."

He turned to go back up the path to the cabin. Donald Gooding was out on his front porch taking his morning cup of coffee. Dan stopped for a quick word regarding breakfast before continuing to the guest cabin where he was staying.

A quick shower followed by a change of clothing later, Dan was back down the path to go with the other pastor to the Canaan resort.

"If it was just me, I'd settle for a bowl of corn flakes in the morning," Pastor Gooding stated when they walked into the resort's dining room. "Your being here gives me an excuse to indulge a little."
"Just so you don't indulge too much," Dan pointed out. "That's why I started running. My indulgences were getting the better of me. Fortunately, I was able to latch onto a running coach."

"Send him my way, won't you?" Pastor Gooding said, looking down at his waist.

"He's a she, moved up from Texas with her boyfriend two years back. The boy runs the local drug store. She's finishing up law school."

"Maybe you can teach me a little while you're here," the pastor suggested.

"I'll think about it," Dan said when they sat down at the breakfast table.

Dan and Pastor Gooding had a wide-ranging conversation at breakfast, occasionally interrupted by staff who knew the local pastor. Dan observed some of the guests in the dining room; a couple on vacation (up from Richmond, he later learned); a small family with a precocious child (reminding him of Grace and Hope), and a man who reminded him of someone he thought he'd seen in and around Magnolia. Every time he tried to get a better look at the other man's face, the other man turned away.

Dan wondered if the other man's aversion was coincidental or intentional.

"Don't be obvious, but there's a man sitting over at a table three rows away from the window," Dan whispered to his host. "Is he someone you've seen before?"

Pastor Gooding spent the better part of a minute maneuvering to get a look at the man Dan asked about.

"Maybe once," he reported. "But then again, I can't be too sure. He might be one of the summer people who show up at services once or twice a year."

"I've seen him, but I can't place him," Dan confided. "It's been recently, too... like within the past two or three weeks."

The stranger seemed to know that he was under observation. He left the dining room with his face turned away from the two pastors.
*****

After breakfast, Dan decided to tarry for a while at the resort while Pastor Gooding went into town to make some calls.

"I'll be back around about four or so to give you a lift back to the house," Pastor told Dan. "If you want to swing back earlier, call me on your cell phone and I can arrange for someone to give you a ride."

Dan took advantage of his situation to do a little bit of walking and listening. He managed to find a path down to the nature center where he had a long discussion about the local flora and fauna with the naturalist. He found curiosities at the gift shop of interest to everyone in his family and nearly exhausted the budget he had set aside for purchasing gifts to bring back home. One of the employees at the nature center mentioned something about heading back to town. Dan asked if he could hitch a ride back to Pastor Gooding's. The employee was only too happy to oblige.

On the way off the resort property, Dan spotted the mystery man from breakfast, hiking along the side of the road headed toward town. For a few moments, he considered asking his driver to double back and offer the man a ride. Another part of him decided that it might be imprudent.

"He has his own life and his own right to privacy," Dan decided. "Besides, it's probably just coincidence."

When he arrived at the guest cabin, he left his host a short message telling him not to bother picking him up. After a quick lunch consisting of a peanut butter sandwich and a glass of tea, he took a short nap followed by a short hike into the nearby woods.

It was glorious.

Dan's mind was in idle for most of the day. He didn't have a flock to worry about or a sermon to write. His church was in good hands. Emily's spiritual revival since moving the family to Magnolia three years earlier was a blessing in more ways than one. She was quite capable of organizing services in the temporary quarters at the high school by herself, and there were always plenty of extra hands available to help.

Pastor Gooding came by the cabin late in the afternoon while Dan was on his hike. He left a note inviting his visitor to dinner at a place south of Canaan Valley Resort.

Dinner was at seven. The evening was pleasant enough for Dan, Donald and Jennifer to sit out on the patio and enjoy a mild breeze. After dinner, Dan decided to drive into Davis to purchase a few items at the grocery store. On his way in, he thought he saw the same man he'd seen that morning at the breakfast buffet.

He thought about approaching the young man to engage in a conversation. By the time he was parked, the man was nowhere to be seen.

"No matter," Dan thought. "Small town. He'll show up again."

Something bothered him about the stranger. He couldn't quite figure out what it was.

Dan drove back to the state park and staked out a place to lay down to stargaze for a while. His only interruption was a phone call from Emily. She had apparently had a rough day. Assuring words were passed. He felt at peace for a while longer. It was just after midnight when he returned to the cabin to go to bed.

Just after six the next morning, he was awakened by someone pounding on the door.

"Dan, Dan Stevens, open up! Deputy Larson from the county sheriff's office!!"

Dan threw on a robe and went to meet the visitor.

There were three.

Pastor Donald Gooding, Deputy Larson and a third man dressed in a jacket with FBI written on it stood on the porch.

"Can you account for your whereabouts last evening after you had dinner with Pastor Gooding?" the deputy demanded.

There was no "hello", no "good morning" – nothing. Just a demand.

Dan's tongue stumbled while he recounted his activities from the previous evening.

"Why? What's the matter?" he concluded.

"Pastor Gooding's church burned down last night," the fellow in the FBI jacket spoke up. "There was a strong odor of gasoline indicating that the fire might have been deliberately set. We understand that your church in Ohio burned down not too long ago."

The horror of watching the Magnolia Community Church go up in flames instantly returned to Pastor Dan.

"We need to run you into the sheriff's office, so we can ask a few questions," the sheriff's deputy told him. "Get dressed. You're coming with me."

Eight

Words of Wisdom, Words of Love

Emily wished that she had had more sleep when she woke up Monday morning. She had trouble getting to sleep because of Vera Mace's appearance at the Sunday evening sing-along.

"THE LORD WILL HAVE HIS VENGEANCE ON YOU, WOMAN!" Miss Mace screamed during the service. "HE KNOWS ABOUT THAT WHORE WHO CAME TO YOUR HOUSE THE MOMENT YOUR HUSBAND WAS GONE! THE WOMAN IS A HARLOT, AND A BABY KILLER! YOU'RE GOING TO HELL FOR HELPING HER DO WHAT SHE'S DONE!"

Thankfully, Mulligan and Chief Richmond were there to remove Vera Mace from the building. It took a few minutes for Emily and the church to settle down so that services could resume. It took a few more minutes for Emily to explain the other woman's outburst and to assure them that Debbie Wallace's miscarriage two years previously wasn't planned, and she wasn't a "Baby Killer".

When she finally did get to sleep, she found herself waking up several times overnight to reach over to the other side of the bed to hold on to the man who wasn't there. In the years they had been married, the only time he wasn't by her side for at least a portion of any given night were those nights when she was in the hospital after having given birth to their children. They were there for each other except very rarely.

At five-thirty, she finally gave in. Since she couldn't sleep, she thought that she may as well do something useful. Emily threw on an old t-shirt and a pair of gym shorts, along with a pair of anklets and running shoes. She thought of putting her shoes to their intended use, but she would rather have a partner to run with. Emily waited on the front porch for a while, hoping that this was one of those mornings when Chloe Thompson would happen by. After about ten minutes of wavering, she enlisted Frank the Dog to watch over the house, so she could take a walk instead.

Emily walked to South Street, intending to make a loop around the town; perhaps taking the time to have a little talk with Tricia Michaels at Zeke's Café. As she neared the intersection of South and Main Streets, she saw Lizzie Elston sitting on the front porch of The Blue and the Gray, dressed in a flimsy nightgown which left little to the imagination. Emily paused momentarily, deciding to join the elderly woman for a minute or two before pressing on.

"You're up mighty early," Lizzie commented as Emily came up on the wide veranda. "Missing your husband?"

"Yes," Emily replied. "Especially after Vera Mace's appearance at services last night."

Lizzie took a sip from a glass of iced tea she had next to her on the arm of her chair.

"That woman has a screw loose," Emily concluded, shaking her head.

Lizzie laughed. "So, the preacher's wife knows the truth! Open up. It'll do you some good."

A fit of laughter overcame Emily. In seconds, Lizzie Elston was laughing as well. Both women finally recovered long enough for Lizzie to ask Emily if she wanted something to drink. The older woman took Emily's order inside, returning with a second glass of tea, this one with a sprig of mint hanging off the side.

"Vera's never been playing with a full deck," Lizzie offered once both women had settled down. "Same could be said about me, too. We all have our idiosyncrasies."

"A fair assessment," Emily agreed. "But we all have reasons for our idiosyncrasies. I'm sure that Vera has her reasons."

"In a word, yes." Lizzie's smile revealed that she knew far more about the absent woman and was about to let Emily in on the secret. "I'm not exactly sure why she feels as she does, but she certainly is committed to making life miserable for you, Daniel, and for that matter, former pastor Kellough, may he rest in peace."

"Maybe Dan's support of your nephew and his partner when we arrived here has something to do with it," Emily reminded her.

"Her recent ravings have more to do with your use of the school as worship space than it does with my nephew," Lizzie told her guest. She then told Emily the story about the tracts Vera left at the school several years earlier. "The woman feels cheated, I suppose," she concluded.

"Could she have caused the fire somehow? Was she investigated?" Emily asked.

"All of us were questioned by the police," Lizzie reminded her. "Everyone with even a remote interest in starting a fire was nowhere near the church when the fire broke out. While I think that Vera would like to have seen the Community Church go up in flames, I doubt that she'd have enough initiative to actually set a fire."

57

"That's what Dan said. It's good to hear it from another source."

Emily took a sip of her tea.

"You know you're in for it today," Lizzie remarked.

"How do you mean?"

"Well, with your husband gone, the people with special needs will be seeking you out to pray for them or to hear a confession," Lizzie pointed out.

"Maybe I should go back to the house." Emily reasoned.

"No need to rush… you're not going to get any company until nine or later." Lizzie shifted position just a bit, so she could look the pastor's wife directly in the eye. "And knowing your children and their ages, you have a good twenty minutes before the youngest, Hope, right?"

Emily nodded to confirm the name of her youngest child.

"Anyway, the youngest tend to be the earliest risers this time of the year."

"I didn't think you knew that," Emily stated. "I was under the impression that you never had kids of your own."

"Never did," Lizzie confessed. "I thought about it, but by the time we were able to do anything about it, it was too late. My time had passed."

"You and Mr. Clark?" Emily asked.

Lizzie nodded. "My parents never approved of the man I loved. We were intimate, but we took precautions."

"Your parents died after you hit menopause."

"That's right," Lizzie confirmed. "Only a few people know about our relationship. If Dr. Jonah Welles found out, I'd have been out of a job, so, we had to keep our secret."

"Surely, others in the school system had to know what was going on," Emily surmised.

"A few board members knew – Bob was even on the board for three terms – but everyone who knew about Bob and me, looked the other way."

"You haven't found the missing plaque yet, have you?" Emily guessed.

"No, I haven't," Lizzie sighed. "There is another, though, at our place in the country. Maybe we can go out there this week, so you can see some of the memories Bob and I had collected over the years."

"I think I might like that," Emily smiled.

"Later this week? Thursday, maybe?" Lizzie inquired.

"Sounds good," Emily agreed.

The women made tentative arrangements to travel to Lizzie's hideaway pending arrangements for the children. After continuing their conversation for another few minutes, Emily excused herself, so she could get back to the parsonage.

Hope was already up when she returned. Her big sister fed her a bowl of cereal.

"I take it you've been out on business," Grace stated as a matter of fact when Emily entered the kitchen. "Whatever am I going to do with you?"

Emily laughed before taking the time to bond with her daughters – an interlude as it worked out – prior to a long and hectic day.

From about nine, onward, there was a steady trickle of petitioners coming to the front door of the Stevens house, each with their own concerns. Some were demanding, some were sorrowful; some sought to give Emily and the family some form of comfort in the absence of her husband.

At mid-afternoon, agent Barada came to the house to lend his support and ask a few questions. This time, she was happy to see him. She felt he had been on the edge of being rude during his previous visit.

"I suppose I might have been on edge the last time I was here," Barada explained. "I'm not supposed to say anything, but the fire at your church resembled similar fires at other churches mostly to the east. Since your husband had ties to a few people back there, the people in charge of <u>that</u> investigation are interested in seeing if there are any similarities."

The agent's explanation worried Emily, but not much.

Her day did go by quickly. Most of the visitors had vanished by the time she needed to start the family dinner. Family time after dinner was mostly peaceful and the girls were in bed by nine-thirty. Jacob and Peter managed to wrangle an invitation for a sleepover with Kevin Peel – one involving a "Snipe Hunt" arranged by Kevin's older step-brother.

*****

After everything had settled down, Emily went out on the front porch to enjoy the warm night air. While Frank settled down next to her, Emily punched a pair of buttons on her cell phone. One of them woke the device, the other, put her in touch with the love of her life. After a couple of soft purrs from the other end, the familiar voice eased its way through the ether, triggering a smile on her face.

"I was hoping that you'd call," Dan Stevens told his wife. "I'd have called myself, but you know how I am with the phone."

"I missed you, too."

"How was your day?"

"The usual, you know, lurching from crisis to crisis with no end in sight," she sighed.

His warm chuckle at her response meant the world to her. She knew that he knew what kind of day she'd had. He often complained about his travails on Mondays.

"I suppose your day was pleasant and stress free," Emily added.

"Actually, it was," Dan confided. "To tell you the truth, I feel majorly guilty about being here without you. Maybe you can leave the kids to your parents and come and join me."

The idea sounded delicious to her. Since moving to Magnolia, they hadn't really had any real quality time together, just the two of them.

"Let me run it past Dad," she told him. "Actually, he suggested that we might want to consider doing just that when we planned the trip."

"Great minds run in the same channel," he quipped.

"Idiots think alike," she shot back.

A moment or two of light laughter later, Dan brought up a more serious note.

"When you come, maybe you can clear up a mystery for me."

He filled her in on his sightings of the mystery man earlier in the day.

"I know I've seen him before, somewhere," he told her. "For some reason, I have this urgent feeling that I need to know who this person is and how he fits into… I don't know… recent events."

"How do you mean?" she asked.

"He might fit into the fire. I know, it seems crazy, but somehow I get the feeling that he is responsible or knows something about who might be."

She waited to hear more from the man she loved.

"I'll try to make arrangements to come over late in the week," she stated, breaking the short silence. "In the meantime, put whatever ills you have out of your mind. I love you."

"I love you, too. Kisses to you, the kids and let everyone know that I'm looking forward to coming back."

"I can't wait."

They both made kissing noises into the phone before hanging up.

Emily went inside and put the phone on the bedside table to allow it to charge. She said a silent prayer then turned off the light, hoping for sleep to take her into its arms and protect her from the day ahead.

If it was anything like the day she'd just completed, she wasn't sure she wanted it to come.

Nine

Deja-Vu All Over Again

The shotgun seat of the FBI agent's government issue Dodge was quite a bit more comfortable than the back seat of the deputy sheriff's Tahoe, at least so Dan Stevens imagined.

"That crazy deputy had it in mind to have you handcuffed," the G-Man remarked. "From the information I got from our man Barada in Ohio, I didn't think that you would be that much of a threat. Pastor Gooding and I practically had to pull teeth to convince him that you'd be around to answer questions."

"You could have let me drive my own car, you know," Dan protested.

"I know, but it is what it is," the G-man pointed out. "Besides, having you with me gives me the chance to yank the sheriff's chain."

Dan considered not having handcuffs as a blessing. He spent the rest of the trip into town without saying a word.

Sheriff George Pinkerman was found at the smoldering ruins of Davis First Baptist, talking with what Dan presumed as the head of the fire department. The G-Man led Dan to the sheriff. The lawman dismissed the fireman then turned his attention to the pastor.

"So, Jimmy – this here's the fellow what burned down the church, right?"

The sheriff talked as if he had a disdain for the G-Man. Dan wondered if it may have had something to do with the color of Jimmy's skin.

"That's James and yes, this is the person you <u>suspect</u> may have had something to do with the church burning down."

63

James got right up in the sheriff's face.

"What you need to know, sheriff is that this man is considered innocent until he can be proved guilty beyond a reasonable doubt. Got that... BOY?"

The sheriff's face turned fifty shades of red.

"Your suspect and I will survey the site while you're adjusting your attitude, Mr. Pinkerman," James declared, walking away. "C'mon, Daniel, let's have a look around."

Dan followed James around the perimeter of the still smoking building. Every few feet, James would stop, examine something, smell the air then continue.

"The fire was started here," he declared at a point where the front door used to be. He held out his arm wavered a little bit, then pointed toward the center of the charred mass.

"It was arson. The arsonist lit the fire here at the entrance. He left a gasoline trail down toward the center of the church in what was most likely the pastor's study. Our investigators will probably find a cache of explosives or accelerants which ignited similar trails through the rest of the church."

"My pastor's study overlooked the parking lot of my church," Dan informed James. "The fire marshal mentioned that there were multiple flash points there, as well."

"Ex-Army," James grunted. "It's just one of several techniques we used when destroying a building. You aren't Army. You didn't do it."

James continued his inspection around the perimeter of the burned-out church, dodging firefighters attending to hot spots.

"Our suspect came in here," James said when they were almost all the way around the building. "He exited the same way then set fire to the building from the outside. From the looks of it, he turned off the gas before he set the fire."

Dan's attention turned to a gas meter. They had walked right past it, him not noticing. He walked back over to the meter, saw that the main supply line was turned to the off position, then walked back over to James.

"How did I miss that?" Dan asked on his return.

"You just did. No big deal," he was told. "It's a further sign that the fire was deliberately set. Whoever did this wanted to burn down the church. Nothing else."

They finished their circuit. Sheriff Pinkerman listened politely to what James had to say, but that was about it. He was obviously upset at having to interact with a man of color.

"I'm taking your suspect to breakfast if you don't mind," James concluded. Before the sheriff could protest, James and Dan were in the G-Man's car.

They stopped three blocks away from the church at a small diner tucked just off the main drag. The place reminded Dan of Zeke's Café back in Magnolia... a throwback to a simpler time where men would gather in the morning before heading off to work.

"Agent Hamner. It's been a while," a man coming out of the kitchen and wearing an apron approached the pair just after they sat down at a small table.

There was a round of acknowledgement in the room. Obviously, James had been there a time or two before. The man in the apron took their orders after serving them coffee

"That was Andy Cremens. He runs this place," James remarked while they were waiting for their meal. "Wish my job brought me here a little more often. Breakfast is to die for."

"Makes up for the sheriff's attitude, I suppose," Dan smiled, taking a sip of coffee.

"He's a throwback. He's not a bad man, just a little backwards about some things. My boss loves to send me here just to rub my presence in his face."

"You're ex-Army?" Dan asked.

"Military Police. Retired. Joined the Bureau the day after I mustered out." James reached for a napkin to catch a bit of coffee he spilled on the table.

"Tell me something about you," James continued. "According to Barada, you were a football star and hell on wheels when you were in school."

"My fame spreads further than I thought it would."

"Barada told me about the relationship you have with the chief of police there in Ohio. Barada told me about the fire at your church. The pattern fit a series of church fires I've been investigating here, in West Virginia, Maryland and Pennsylvania. Mostly non-denominational or Baptist, smaller communities and white.

"Anyway, according to Barada, you have a wife, four kids and a church you're barely keeping up with. I always heard that the Lord works in mysterious ways."

66

"I feel flattered, but at the same time, I'm more than just a little concerned," Dan said, moving closer to the G-Man. "It's almost as if there's a dossier on me out there."

"Truthfully, yes, there is," James confided. "We share little bits of information now and then about people of interest. Barada told me to look out for you while you were here. He sent over your dossier and I read it. I was going to find some excuse to meet you for lunch today or tomorrow to pick your brain. I suspect that there is some sort of connection between you and the fire back in Ohio. The fact that you are here when there's another church fire has raised an eyebrow or two.

"It's just like I told you. It was done by or looks like it was done by someone who'd been in the Army. According to the information I have, you don't have the background to have set the fire the way it was set. There's a specialist in this sort of thing coming up from D.C. this morning to confirm my observations. In the meantime, the jackass with the sheriff's uniform needs assurance that I'm keeping a close eye on his number one suspect."

"But he doesn't trust you."

"He doesn't trust you, either, but he's afraid to cross me for fear of losing his job. It's… complicated. We're involved in an elaborate dance, that's all. Once my expert comes in, you'll be in the clear."

"Let's hope so," Dan mumbled.

"It'll be alright," James assured him. "I'll see that some of the pressure's taken off. My daddy was a pastor. I know what it can do to a man."

"So, you understand?"

"Daddy said that there were times when he felt like he was getting fired on from all sides," James explained. "Nothing he could say or do would please everyone. He was filled with doubts, beset with depression and in need of prayer almost all the time. There were times when he doubted the existence of God, when he lost his faith in God, in humanity, even himself.

"Mama would beg him to go away, get lost for a while, take time off. He never did. My daddy died at the age of fifty-five of a heart attack caused by the stress he endured by his profession. He was a good man, Daniel Stevens. Just like you; a good man."

"What if I snapped?" Dan speculated. "What if somehow I did manage to burn down my own church and Pastor Gooding's for good measure?"

"It's within the realm of possibility, pastor," James replied, "but not very likely. Like I just told you, you don't have the background to have set this fire, at least, the way it was set."

Doubt started to creep back into the back of Dan's mind. While James tried to lighten the mood by talking about the history of the area, Dan looked listlessly out the front window of the restaurant, watching and wondering if the life he had known was coming to an end.

It came in a flash, then disappeared.

Dan sat bolt upright and urged James to twist around and look out the window.

"What is it?" the G-Man asked.

"I saw him – that guy. He was at breakfast at the lodge yesterday morning. He just went by. I saw him!"

James signaled the owner to let him know to hold their breakfasts until they returned. The pair went out the front door to look up and down the street, only to find that there was no one around.

"He was here! Just a moment ago, he was here in front of the restaurant!" There was no one there.

James did a quick sweep of the area, looking for signs of Dan's sighting.

"If there was someone here, he left in a mighty big hurry," James declared.

"Look here." James picked up a still-smoldering cigarette butt and showed it to Dan.

"Do you see where he might have gone? Did you get a good look at him?" James asked.

"No and no," Dan stated. "I saw him yesterday morning at the dining room at the lodge… at least I caught a glimpse of his face… but he hid, as if he didn't want to be seen, especially by me."

"Can you describe him?"

James pulled a notebook out of his shirt pocket.

"Male, white, maybe late twenties, early thirties. Six foot, maybe. One seventy-five."

"If I brought in a sketch artist, could you recall enough detail, so we could get a good idea what this man of yours looks like?"

Dan nodded. "Maybe," he said. "I don't think that I'd be very helpful, though."

"You might be more help than you know," Agent Hamner told his guest. "If you can help us identify this mystery man you saw, you might be able to help me break this case wide open."

Ten

Troubled Dreams – Troubled Reality

Emily's dreams were troubled. They were at first, peaceful. Then there was fire, confusion and the form of someone running away. She knew who it was but could not put a name to the face. She had seen before.

She woke up in a cold sweat at five-fifteen. Something wasn't quite right. She couldn't put her finger on it, but something wasn't quite right. She lay in bed for the next two hours catching occasional bits of sleep before finally giving up.

Emily Stevens had just gone downstairs to turn on the morning news when the phone rang.

"Emily Stevens, this is Rob Barada. I hate to bother you so early in the morning, but there's been another church fire… this time in West Virginia."

A wave of dread swept over Emily while the agent continued.

"I recall you saying something about you sending your husband there. Where was he going?"

"He went to visit his old college roommate at his place just outside Davis West Virginia. Dan left right after Sunday morning services."

"That's probably why the Tucker County Sheriff is looking for him."

Emily's heart sank to her knees. "Please Lord, keep him safe," she prayed silently.

"He seems to think that your husband may have set a church on fire based on an anonymous tip."

Silence.

"Mrs. Stevens… Mrs. Stevens…"

Fear started to take hold of Emily's heart.

"Can I call you back?" she finally said to the Agent.

"Of course," he told her.

She hung up the phone, filled with doubt; filled with fear.

Dan had been showing signs of needing something she just couldn't put her finger on. She had training in the art of counseling, yet she couldn't apply that training when it came to her husband.

It was just like what happened to her Uncle Mike. Mike was driving with Emily's Aunt Susan when he pulled over to the side of the Interstate, suffered a heart attack and died. Susan was a registered nurse with her CPR certification. She could have kept her husband alive until an ambulance arrived to take him to a hospital. Instead, she froze. Helpless. By the time help arrived it was too late.

Emily found that she was now facing a similar crisis.

Dan showed signs of depression, of not being able or willing to carry on his duties at the Community Church. Emily saw the signs yet felt helpless. Unable to do anything about it, even though she was becoming equipped to be able to help.

Hope wandered into the kitchen clutching her favorite toy – a stuffed dog she called Roger. She put Roger on the kitchen table before sitting down herself in expectation of a bowl of cereal.

"Where's Daddy?" Hope asked.

"He's taking time off. He's out of town," Emily answered.

"Why?"

"He needs it."

"Why?"

"He works very hard and loves a lot of people," Emily tried to explain to Hope.

"Why?"

"It's his job, that's why."

Hope seemed content with the answer. She waited until Emily served her bowl of cereal before speaking again.

"Do you have a job, Mommy?"

"I have a job. A very important job. I take care of you."

She emphasized the point by touching Hope on the nose.

"You take care of Roger?" Hope said, holding up her stuffed dog.

"Taking care of Roger is your job, just like Gracie takes care of Frank."

"Why?"

"It is the way it is, Hope," Emily explained while sitting down with a bowl of cereal for herself. "Each one of us helps each other. It's called loving your neighbor."

"Like Mrs. Larson?"

"Like Mrs. Larson."

Hope paused to think, before eating her cereal. She finished, placed her bowl in the sink, gathered Roger then started to walk toward the living room. She stopped.

"I'm glad we had this talk," Hope stated as a matter of fact.

"Me, too," Emily assured her.

Maybe she was assuring herself.

At a quarter till eight, Gracie came downstairs preceded by Frank the Dog. Frank headed to the back door to let him out. He came back in at about the same time Jacob and Peter came back with Kevin and his mother. The kitchen erupted in a flurry of cereal boxes, bowls, spoons and milk.

While breakfast was in full swing, Emily excused herself to quietly steal to Dan's downstairs study to call Jaybo Hatfield.

"Jaybo, Dan may be in trouble. I got a call from Rob Barada of the FBI this morning. There was a church burning last night somewhere near where Dan was staying."

"And they suspect him?" Jaybo asked.

"I was told that there was an anonymous tip," she told him. "Given what we've been talking about, could it be possible that he's snapped and become an arsonist?"

"Anything's possible, but not necessarily probable. Arsonists tend to have problems other than what we've been discussing about Dan."

"I thought so. I wanted to be sure," Emily said. "It's just that I'm worried."

"Wait it out," Jaybo prescribed. "Give it a day. If there was a tip like you said, chances are that the police would figure out sooner than later that they've reached a dead end. In my opinion, the cops would be better off looking for the tipster. Find the tipster and you'll have a much better idea who might have started the fire."

"Is there even the remotest of a possibility that Dan may have started either fire?"

A feeling of dread gripped Emily again.

"There is that possibility," Jaybo conceded. "I don't sense it, but there is that possibility."

They conversed in general for another few minutes. Jaybo volunteered to come to visit Emily later that day.

"If you don't mind, I could use the help," she told him.

"Maybe some therapy; you and the kids," he suggested, "Would you consider come out to the farm with the kids for a visit later this week?"

"I'm not sure..." she hesitated.

"It might do you and your kids good," he offered. "We're having people over on Friday for a swim down at the swimming hole behind the house, followed by a cookout."

Emily had heard stories about the swimming hole Jaybo was talking about. It was a place where the locals in and around Jumpstart would go and skinny dip. Before Hope, she would have taken their children down to the hole to let them splash and play to their hearts' content. Since moving to Magnolia, her three older children had outgrown naked romps in the backyard sprinkler afforded by living out in the country. They still slept naked but had gotten used to dressing before leaving their rooms in the morning.

Emily took a deep breath. "I... think I'll have to give it a pass."

"Give what a pass, Mom?"

Jacob had somehow wrested himself away from the activities going on in the family room.

"We'll talk later, Jacob," she told him.

"Sorry, Jaybo," she returned to her conversation with the counselor. "The boys are getting to a certain age, you know."

"I understand," he replied. "Let's talk later, okay?"

Emily agreed before heading back to the kitchen to clean up the morning dishes. She was surprised to see Jacob's friend, Jaclyn standing next to her son, helping him clean up.

"Oh, hi, Mom," Jacob perked up when he noticed his mother. "I was going to tell you that Jaclyn came here while you were on the phone."

"I see that you've decided to let her help you get ahead on your chores," Emily smiled. She knew that her son was anxious about spending time with his friend. He was also out to impress the girl.

"It's okay, Mrs. Stevens. I'm glad to be able to help," Jaclyn chipped in.

Emily sat down at the kitchen table while the pair of teenagers made a game of finishing the breakfast dishes. Emily's mind drifted back to her first boyfriend, a quiet kid from church named Eric. He was a year older than she was, but not quite ready for her advances. She enlisted her father's help in inviting the boy over to their house to spend time at a cookout and a have a swim in the backyard pool.

Emily was determined to make Eric the first boy she kissed on the lips. She remembered the day. It was warm and sunny. She went with her father out to Eric's house to pick him up. Her father squeezed them both in one seat belt on the front seat of their red Nova. Eric squirmed while Emily tried to think of how she could steal that kiss. Since he was about to go into the eighth grade and she into the seventh, he must have already had experience.

That was part of what seventh graders did – have their first kiss with someone of the opposite sex.

When they arrived, Eric was almost immediately shuffled into her bedroom to change into his swimsuit while she changed into hers in the bathroom. The thought of a boy naked in her bedroom was somehow exciting for her. They arrived in the back yard at almost the same time. There was some back and forth before they were playing innocent games in the small above-ground pool. Eventually she had him right where she wanted. Emily stole her first kiss from Eric. In front of her parents, too.

The rest of that afternoon was anti-climactic. Emily had a hard time trying to figure out why Eric didn't seem as thrilled as she was about their kiss, or why he didn't try for another one while he was there.

"Boys reach their emotional maturity later in life than girls do," her mother later explained. "Give him another year or two. He'll most likely come around."

Eric and his family moved away before he was old enough to give Emily a proper kiss.

A smile coursed across Emily's face while she watched her son and a girl with the same hopes and dreams as she did when she was her age wash dishes together.

Jacob had no idea what was in store for him.

Her whiff of nostalgia was interrupted by the jarring ring of the telephone. Jacob picked it up.

"For you, Mom," he said.

She picked up the receiver.

"Rob Barada, again. Just thought I'd let you know that your husband is safe for the moment. He's with the agent working on the case in West Virginia. No charges have been filed, but, the agent told me that the local sheriff is getting antsy."

"He will be kept safe, right?" Emily asked.

"Our agent on the scene will do his best, although the sheriff has been known to bend rules to get his way," Agent Barada reported. "I'll pass along your phone number so an agent on the scene can be in contact. I'll touch base with you periodically, too. Don't worry. Dan Stevens is in good hands."

Eleven

Meeting Agent Beasley

After breakfast in town, FBI Agent James Hamner took Dan Stevens back to his temporary home away from home. He waited on the front porch while the pastor showered and made himself presentable.

"We still have a while before the artist I've called in arrives. While you were in the shower, I called agent Barada. He's been in contact with your wife. I'll call her myself later. In the meantime, let me tell you what I'm up against – what we're up against."

James waited for Dan to get comfortable, or at least as comfortable as one could get on the cold metal chairs on the front porch of the cabin, before starting his story.

"I've been investigating a series of church fires in three... scratch that... five states here in the past eighteen months. The fires happen at small, either Baptist or non-denominational churches in small towns in rural counties."

"Barada mentioned church fires," Dan interrupted.

"The fires getting the publicity are fires set at predominately black churches. The fires I'm investigating have all been set in churches with predominantly white congregations," James explained. "At first, it was thought that the pastors of those churches were all under stress to the point where burning down their church seemed to be a logical choice to ease the pressure. I was called in because of my father. The Bureau thought that I might be in a unique position to investigate.

"One of the first things I noted was the pattern. All the fires seemed to start in the pastor's study before rapidly spreading to the rest of the church. Well, the Bureau was right; I was in a unique position, but it was because of my experience in the Army, not because of the sins of my father.

"Every time there was another fire, we spent hours interviewing pastors and just about anyone else we could think of. Other than appearing to be set by someone who knows what he or she is doing, there was no other common connection on any of the fires – until now."

"I'm the only pastor who's been in the area at more than one fire, I take it," Dan remarked.

"You're the only pastor who is known to have been in the area at more than one fire," James affirmed. "That makes you suspect, except for the fact that you've pretty much stayed in Magnolia ever since you arrived to take over and not having the training to set the fires in the way they were set."

"Bob Barada did a pretty thorough job of talking with just about everyone in town," Dan told the agent. "I doubt that someone from Magnolia would have been involved. It's a pretty close community. When someone sneezes at one end of town, there's a chorus of blessings starting from the other."

"That's something else the fires have in common. They've all been in small, tight knit communities where everyone knows everyone else. You're the outsider, and since the same thing happened at your church, the sheriff here is ready to judge you guilty and have you thrown in jail just based on your being here."

"How did he know so quickly?" Dan asked.

"He got an anonymous tip while the fire was at its peak. It might have been phoned in by your man – the one we stopped and looked for at the restaurant."

A signal on Agent Hamner's cell phone interrupted their conversation. He looked at a text message then responded.

"That was Beasley, my sketch artist. She just got into town. I told her to come up here. She'll be here in half an hour," James told Dan. "Can I hit the john while we're waiting?"

Dan waited while Agent Hamner took care of some personal business. When he returned, he gave Dan some background information while waiting for Beasley.

James' father had been an Episcopal priest in a New York parish. His son described him as being full of joy on the outside but filled with inner demons. The father's death was not altogether unexpected. He fought off his depression with food, ignoring his chronic high blood pressure and a few other borderline health problems.

"I loved my Dad," James admitted. "I've determined to help other pastors by giving them my support in my off time. This assignment marks the first time where my career and my passion have come together."

"What's my passion? What's my career? Are they one and the same?" The questions swirled around in Dan's head while James went in a different direction.

Beasley arrived shortly before eleven. She was a petite woman, no more than five-three, wearing a head of thick, black short cropped hair. She appeared carrying a laptop and a portable printer in addition to a case containing artist's supplies.

James stayed while Dan gave Beasley as much information as he could about the man he'd seen. Within a few minutes, she came up with a reasonable sketch which she then scanned into her laptop. She showed Dan her drawing, so he could have a good look at the face.

"That's a remarkable resemblance to the man I saw," Dan said after carefully examining Beasley's work.

She smiled at the compliment then posted the sketch she scanned over the internet. Since it was lunchtime, Dan suggested they go grab a bite to eat, a suggestion both agents readily agreed upon. Beasley suggested a place further down the valley, a pizza joint called B. J's.

They drove in two cars. Beasley drove ahead of James, turning into the dirt and gravel parking lot where only three other cars were parked at the time. Once they stopped, Dan got out while James stayed to take a call on his cell phone. Beasley motioned for Dan to follow her into the restaurant.

B. J's was just one of several restaurants in the valley which relied on the tourist trade. In the winter, skiers from two different resorts would flood the place with talk of winter sports and conditions on the slopes. In summer, people came from the metropolitan areas on the east coast to escape the heat. B. J's was in the summer mode, meaning most of their business came from families looking for relatively inexpensive family fare.

Dan and Beasley placed an order for a pair of pepperoni pizzas and three drinks then sat down for light conversation.

There was something unsettling about her. If she was a member of his congregation, there would have been no problem. Anything she said or did which would have attracted him to her would have been filtered through his love for his wife, his love for his children and his sense of duty to provide a member of his congregation with a safe and confidential relationship. In this setting, he felt himself being drawn to her like a moth to a flame. He wasn't sure of why she attracted him. Her mannerisms? The way she spoke? Her laugh?

He made a point about telling her about his children hoping to dispel his increasing interest in the agent. No matter how hard he tried, he still felt a strong attraction to this woman who came into his life less than an hour earlier. Somehow, she seemed not to care about the other aspects of his life. She continued to weave her spell on him until James came to join them at the table.

"Barada's been on the phone with the sheriff's office," he informed them. "He's having trouble trying to convince the sheriff that you have a clean bill of health. I need to get over to Parsons and get the sheriff straightened out before he decides to send a posse to arrest you."

"I wish you could stay at least for a little bit and pour your drink," Dan suggested.

"I need to get going," James told them. "You two can wait at the cabin when you're finished here. I'll be up later this afternoon once I've had a talk with the sheriff and the county judge."

James paused just long enough to take his empty cup over to the soft drink machine and fill it before heading out the door.

For a fleeting moment, Dan thought about asking his new friend to take him along to see the sheriff. His attraction to Beasley held him back.

"You're worried," she said once James left. "It's me, isn't it?"

Dan wasn't sure how to respond. Yes, it was her. He was afraid that she might try to lure him away from his family, yet, part of him needed to be lured away.

"It's not you, it's something else."

It was her. He told a lie… or was it a fib? The chain of events was momentarily interrupted by the entrance of a couple with their two small children.

"Don't hit your sister… Jesus sees you hitting your sister, and he doesn't like it!"

The mother was no older than he was. She was at least fifty pounds overweight and seemed to lord her size over her charges. The husband quietly assented to the woman's demands on her suffering children. Dan was reminded of Jacob and Peter at that age. They would occasionally have minor tiffs with each other, but both he and Emily were able to get the boys to settle their difficulties with patience and a dose of love.

The husband and his children placed their order while the mother pulled out her cell phone. She didn't want to participate in her children's lives. That was obvious. She didn't wish to be inconvenienced.

"I like to go hiking up here."

Beasley placed herself directly in Dan's attention.

"How far is your cabin from the ridge trail?"

"A quarter mile, maybe," he replied. "If you have the time, I can take you up when we leave here."

Emily wouldn't mind. She could trust him. Beasley could trust him. The only person who might not be able to trust Dan Stevens was Dan Stevens. Still, he opened his mouth and the invitation came stumbling out.

"Go get me my drink. Get me a Diet Coke!"

The woman's demand came just moments before her husband was about to sit down. She continued talking on her cell phone, ignoring her own children. Dan looked over to see if he could make eye contact with the husband – to perhaps let him know that things would get better. Jacob and Peter grew out of their combative stage. Certainly, the two children kicking each other's shins under the table would grow into a more loving stage.

"I brought my hiking boots, my staff and some hiking clothes with me," Beasley told the pastor. "Maybe we could go on a short hike after lunch."

Now he was committed. He didn't really want to be, but he was committed to hiking into the woods with a woman other than his wife. He wondered if maybe James would be willing to be a chaperone. Did he really need a chaperone? He stared off into space. More properly, he watched as the family situation at the newcomer's table deteriorate just as surely as he thought his marriage would go down the drain because of Beasley.

"I was up awfully early," Dan tried to excuse himself. "I may want to take a nap instead."

"That's okay," Beasley assured him. "I have work to do. I can wait on your front porch, get done what has to be done, then go off on my own if you're still napping."

There was no escape. The woman was going to be his bodyguard until questions about the fire in Davis could be answered.

"I can see by the look on your face that you are uncomfortable." Beasley furrowed her eyebrows then put her hands, palms up on the table in front of Dan. "There's no need. I have no grand designs other than to keep an eye on you. Because of the situation, you can't be left alone. I'm sorry. It has to be this way."

Dan was about to say something directly to her when their pizzas arrived. Beasley asked the server to box their order to go. Just as the pizzas left the table, Dan caught sight of someone else coming in the front door.

"It's him!"

Before either of them could react, the newcomer was back out the door and sprinting across the parking lot. Dan ran to the door and watched as the stranger jumped on a motorcycle and roared out of the gravel parking lot in a trail of dust. Beasley came up behind Dan.

"That's the guy?" she asked.

"That's the guy," he confirmed.

"Did you happen to catch what he was riding?"

"It was a motorcycle. Someone's V – Twin, I guess."

"Go back in and get the pizzas," she told him. "I need to report this."

Dan met the bewildered server, collected the pizzas and the drinks then met Beasley at her car.

"We don't have much to go on," Beasley reported. "The state police have been notified, but…"

Dan heard it, too. There was a roar coming down the road heading in the same direction as the man who'd just been in B. J's. A large group of motorcycles roared past, each of them emitting an ear-splitting roar as they passed by.

Dan looked back at the restaurant. He saw a couple of small faces glued to one of the windows, watching the parade go by.

"At least they've gotten a break from having to listen to their mother," Dan remarked while he got in the car.

When he was settled in, Beasley had him hold the pizza boxes on his lap for the ride back to the cabin. The warmth and the aroma took him back to his childhood. Saturday night was pizza night at the Stevens household. Dan remembered going with his father to the pizza place in Prentiss, then riding back home with the fresh, warm pizzas in his lap.

"Those days are gone," he sighed to himself. He could walk to Father Linguini's with Jacob or Peter, but it just wasn't the same. He thought about going to the pizza place he remembered in Prentiss, but by the time he moved back to Magnolia with his family, the place in Prentiss was gone.

He looked over to Beasley. She was intent on getting Dan back to the cabin where he'd be protected. She was on a mission. Images of a possible romantic interlude with this woman disappeared from his mind when he came to the realization that she wasn't playing games. She was on a mission – to keep him from potential harm.

Twelve

On Pins and Needles

Emily's day became increasingly hectic. Tuesdays weren't supposed to be that way. There were the usual chores which needed attention. Eventually, word leaked out about the fire in West Virginia and Dan's possible involvement. The news prompted a stream of visitors to the parsonage, interrupting the flow of what Emily would normally be doing. With Dan gone, she had the additional burden of having to take care of church business as well.

She tried several times to contact her husband to no avail. His cell phone kept telling her that he was unavailable. Dan had the habit of forgetting his phone from time to time, especially when he wanted to be out of reach. She recalled his disappearance on several occasions since the move to Magnolia, but in each instance, police chief Harold Richmond knew exactly where he could be found.

Harold came by to visit just before lunch saving Emily the bother of making the call.

"What's this I hear about there being another church bombing over near where Dan's staying," he asked when she answered the door.

"Unless you've heard from the FBI, you know about as much as I do," Emily stated. "I was hoping he'd at least call to tell me something, but so far, I've heard nothing."

"I haven't heard a peep out of Dan since he left the other day," the policeman informed her. "I was hoping that he would at least give you a call."

"The only news I've heard is that there's an investigation about the fire and that the sheriff in West Virginia suspects Dan," she sighed. "The only reason he's not sitting in a jail cell is that he's under the protection of the Bureau. I'm not sure what I should do."

"Tell you what… let me rattle a few cages and see if I can find out more about the situation. I'm sure that at least one of my contacts has an idea of what's happening."

Emily agreed to let Harold find out what was going on, freeing her up to take care of her family.

After Harold left, she closed her eyes and crossed her hands in front of her bosom. "Please, God, look after my Dan… and please look after the people who had been affected by the fire in West Virginia. And please, touch the heart of whoever did the deed and lead them to the right path. In Jesus' name, Amen."

Soon after offering up her prayer, Hope came to be with her mother. "I miss Daddy," she said plainly.

"I miss him, too," Emily answered her child.

"Is that why you're so sad?"

"Yes, dear."

Emily cradled her youngest child in her arms then took her out to the porch swing. Several neighbors walked by and remarked on how much Hope had grown. Emily smiled. It seemed like only yesterday she would nurse the infant Hope on that very swing. The neighbors were used to seeing the pair engaged in the natural act of feeding. They all accepted the mother and daughter. Everyone, that is, except for Vera Mace.

"The woman has no shame," Lizzie Elston told Emily after Vera raised the first fuss about nursing Hope on the front porch. "Then there are times like this where she feels it is her duty to be the morality police."

Grace came out with Frank the Dog a few minutes later.

"Your phone was ringing," She told her Mother.

"Did you bring it from the kitchen table?" Emily asked, knowing the answer.

"I was hoping to talk to your Father."

"No, it's still there. I'll go get it."

Grace ran back into the house, letting the screen door slam behind her when she went in. Less than a minute later, she came back out to hand the phone to her mother. Emily gave a quick look to see if the missed call came from Dan. The caller left a voice mail.

"Your husband's going to get what's coming to him," said a muffled voice on the phone.

Emily was taken aback.

Someone appeared to be threatening her. She wasn't sure, so, she called Agent Barada.

"Let me call Hamner," the agent advised. "We'll get someone down there to keep an eye on you."

Emily waited no more than fifteen minutes. FBI agent James Hamner called to assure her that he would do everything in his power to protect her and her husband. He told her that he was in touch with Dan, and that they had been to Davis to view the burnt-out church. "I'll help get him through this, ma'am," the agent assured her. "For now, God's in charge. I'll call when we find out more."

Something about the agent's voice gave Emily peace. Her peace was interrupted by the phone and a restless Hope.

"I just got a call from the FBI."

Emily expected a call from Harold, but not so soon. "Hey, Harold," she answered. "I just got a call from an agent over in West Virginia. He seems to think that the situation is under control."

"That's the way I heard it, too," Harold affirmed. "Do you need to head over there? We can hold down the fort."

"I'm going to wait this out a little bit," she told him. "I don't think there's anything to whatever Dan is being accused of doing for one thing. For another, if I were to go over, I wouldn't go until after Wednesday evening Bible study."

Emily thought about telling him about the anonymous phone threat but didn't, thinking it would only cause the police chief more worry than he already had. She thanked Harold for his concern then went inside to get her girls situated so she could get more of her chores done.

Emily's mother breezed in not long after she started a load of laundry. "You need to be with him," Mrs. Griswold admonished her daughter. "Your father and I will take care of the children. You can take our car. Just go."

Emily tried to convince her mother that she couldn't "just go" and that she wouldn't go at least for another forty-eight hours. "I have obligations here other than the children," she pointed out.

"Your father and Mulligan can conduct Wednesday services," her mother countered. "Your husband needs you. Go."

She finally allowed Grace and Hope to go with their grandmother, telling her mother that it would take her a few hours to arrange for the trip. There was a truce, albeit temporary. The girls and Frank left the house to go down the street to stay while Emily made motions of starting to pack.

She didn't get very far along in her preparations before the next wave of phone calls started. For a full hour, she was bombarded with calls from nearly everyone she knew and people she didn't know quite as well. Most of her friends urged her to go immediately.

Except one.

Lizzie Elston showed up at Emily Stevens' door shortly after noon.

"Don't go until you have good reason to go," Lizzie told her. "Dan can manage whatever situation he's involved in."

"But I'm almost packed," Emily protested.

"No, you aren't." Lizzie was firm. She sat Emily down and continued. "Your mother called me right after she got back to the shop. She had second thoughts."

"Why didn't she say anything to me?" Emily was confused.

"She didn't want to hurt your feelings, for one, and for another, Dan might be in a situation where you'd be better off at home – holding down the fort, so to speak. It's like I said. Dan can manage."

"But…"

"But nothing. You can help me clear something up right here in Magnolia. It'll keep your mind off what's happening in West Virginia."

93

Thirteen

Putting Things in Order

A sheriff's cruiser blocked the driveway leading to the cabin where Dan was staying. Beasley pulled right up to the deputy perched on the car's fender. "What's going on here, Rusty?" she asked.

"Sorry, Beasley," the deputy apologized. "But I have strict orders to be on the lookout for Dan Stevens. I'm to detain the prisoner and take him back to the sheriff's office."

"This is Mr. Stevens and Mr. Stevens will stay with me," Beasley told the deputy, "that is unless you can produce a proper warrant."

"Well, he has a warrant waiting in Parsons…"

"That's not good enough, Rusty," she interrupted. "Unless you have a warrant in your hand, you may not have Mr. Stevens."

The deputy stood dumbfounded.

"You know the rules, now move the car and let us through. Our pizza's getting cold," Beasley demanded.

Rusty shook his head and moved his cruiser. Beasley continued up the driveway.

"You know him, I take it," Dan remarked.

"Rusty Collier and I go way back," she told him. "We'd arm wrestle back in grade school. I always bested him, too."

"And he ended up here? How ironic."

"Rusty didn't as much end up here as he ended up staying here. We've known each other for most of our lives," Beasley told Dan.

"I thought you might be on a first name basis."

"Nobody uses my first name. Everyone knows me as Beasley."

She parked her car next to his, continuing to talk while they got out of the car.

"Even my Daddy calls me Beasley. Everyone but my mother calls me Beasley. She was the only one who called me by my first name."

"What is it... your first name, that is."

"You'll have to ask my mother," she told him while they entered the cabin. "But I don't think that you'll get her to talk with you. She's buried outside of Parsons."

"I'm sorry to hear that," Dan told her.

"It's alright," Beasley sighed. "That was years ago. Let's eat."

They went inside. Beasley took the pizza boxes from Dan, set them on the table in the front room, opened them then started to dig in. Dan offered a short prayer which she pointedly ignored – walking over the refrigerator to look for something to drink while holding a piece of pizza.

"Beer?" she said, looking puzzled. "I was led to understand that you were a minister."

"I am," he told her. "But that doesn't keep me from an occasional beer."

"But you're supposed to preach against it, aren't you? I mean, the evils of John Barleycorn and the temptations of evil?"

"I preach against the overconsumption of alcohol, not total abstinence. A little now and then can actually be beneficial," Dan pointed out. "Too much of anything can be harmful, even water."

"So, you don't mind if I steal one of your beers."

"Not at all. Grab me a pop while you're in there, would you?"

Beasley brought a can of cola and a can of beer to the table and sat down.

"I take it you don't care for preachers," Dan probed.

"I've seen enough snake handlers and holy rollers in my lifetime to think that there's something fundamentally wrong with Christianity."

"Same here," he agreed.

"Are you a preacher or are you not a preacher?" she asked.

"Part of the reason I'm here is to sort that out."

"You believe in something, don't you – like a road to salvation through your personal belief, or something?"

"The question of salvation is moot. It's something in the future," he pointed out. "It's based on if there's really an afterlife."

"Do you believe there is an afterlife?" Beasley asked.

"It depends on your belief system. There are plenty of different beliefs out there; every one of them is valid to the people who believe in them."

Beasley broke into a broad smile.

"Even Wicca?" she asked.

"Even Wicca," Dan confirmed. "It fills a human need to belong or to believe in something larger than one's self."

"I'm Wiccan," Beasley confessed. "Does that challenge what you might think of me personally?"

"At one time, it might have. Now I'm not so sure. I've seen a lot of positive energy from people who identify themselves as Wiccan."

"Don't you think I'll go to hell if I'm not a Christian?"

Dan smiled.

"What happens to you at the end of your life depends in what you believe. You have a belief system which works for you and that's all that's important, now isn't it?"

"I never thought I'd hear that from a fundie," she admitted. "Almost makes me want to go to church."

"Well, if you're ever in Magnolia, you're welcome to attend.

"Would you mind shifting gears here for a few minutes?" he continued. "I'd like to know if I need to get ready to go to jail. Will we be able to finish our lunch?"

"More than likely, yes. We can finish lunch," Beasley assured him. She paused to chew the mouthful of pizza she'd just taken. "As far as keeping you out of jail, even for a little bit, will depend. Time will determine what happens. Takes the better part of an hour to get to the county seat and another hour just to get back. Then there's the Judge. He'll need to issue an order. If he's pre-disposed, it'll still take him an hour just to get the paperwork together. I really don't see him or a deputy back here before, say, five or so."

"So, I could probably get in a nap," Dan said.

"You go right ahead," Beasley assured him. "I'll be close in case anything happens."

*****

They finished their meal then cleaned up what little needed to be cleaned up. Dan went into the cabin's small bedroom while Beasley went out onto the front porch. Because of the busy morning, Dan fell asleep easily.

"We need to get up. Sheriff's on his way."

Beasley's voice cut through a hazy dream Dan had about having to write a sermon on some subject he knew nothing about. He opened his eyes to see Beasley drying herself. She had obviously been taking advantage of the hot tub on the back porch.

"Rusty just gave me a heads-up. Sheriff has a warrant to arrest you and search your car," she explained. "We have three minutes before he gets here if we're lucky."

"And if we're not?" Dan was coming out of the haze of his after-lunch nap.

"Less than a minute."

She dropped her towel exposing her backside to him and then marched out of the bedroom onto the back porch where she got dressed. Beasley didn't seem the least bit concerned about exposing herself. Dan felt guilty for invading her personal space, and even more guilty about a hint he had of arousal.

He got up and headed to the front of the cabin just in time to see a parade of three sheriff's patrol cars, lights flashing, making their way up the driveway. Beasley came up behind him, using his shoulder as a brace while she put on one of her shoes.

"At least we had a minute and a half," she sighed.

The cars stopped in unison. The sheriff and five of his deputies got out of their cars. Two of the deputies stood next to Dan's car while the sheriff and the other three deputies marched right up to the cabin door. Beasley opened the door before the sheriff could knock on it.

"Stand aside, ma'am," the sheriff told Beasley. "I have business with Mr. Stevens."

He pushed her aside before she could object.

"Mr. Daniel Lee Stevens," the sheriff glared, "Please hand over your car keys."

"The keys are in it. It's unlocked."

One of the deputies called out the same fact at almost the same time.

"Been expecting us?" the sheriff asked.

Dan shrugged his shoulders.

"Let me cut to the chase, son."

The sheriff was through being polite.

"You are the primary suspect in the arson of the First Baptist Church in Davis. You are under arrest..."

Dan stood in shock, unable to move while his Miranda rights were being read. The world seemed to slow down. He looked over at Beasley, hoping that she would say something which would make the sheriff go away so he could finish his nap, have dinner and wait for the next morning when everything would return to normal.

He was led outside, told to put his hands on one of the patrol cars and spread his legs so that he could be frisked. To keep his mind off the fact that he was being violated, he looked over to his car – his wife's car - as deputies opened every door. Just as he was told to get up and led to the back seat of a patrol car, the deputy searching the trunk summoned the sheriff over to see something. They spoke in hushed tones. The sheriff just nodded his head then barked some orders. Rusty and another deputy got in the front seat of the patrol car, backed it up, turned around and headed back down the driveway.

"Judge ain't goin' to be too happy with you when sheriff shows him the evidence we just found in your trunk," Rusty commented when they turned onto the main road. "The way it looks, you better have a damn good lawyer, preacher. A damn good lawyer."

With the phone calls and the comings and goings of everyone, Emily almost forgot about her eldest son and a girlfriend doing the breakfast dishes without being asked.

It dawned on her that there might be something suspicious about the deal.

Her suspicions came out of the back of her mind at just about the time Jacob came in the front door.

Alone.

"Hi, mom," he said, almost casually, while sprinting up the stairs to his room.

"Hold on there a minute, mister," Emily commanded. "Didn't I see you in the company of a certain young lady earlier this morning?"

He stopped in the middle of the stairway.

"Well, yeah," he said. "But she had something in mind to do today which I didn't like the sound of. Can I go on up to my room?"

"What did she have in mind?" Emily asked.

"Well, this friend of hers and her boyfriend were going to drive up to something they called the swimming hole somewhere out in the county."

"You know how to swim," Emily reminded her son.

She hesitated for just a moment then asked, "This swimming hole. Would it be out near a place called Jumpstart?"

"You've heard of it, then," Jacob said.

"Yes, I've heard of it," she confirmed. "It's behind the Hatfield's place about a mile out of Jumpstart. We've been invited to go out there later this week."

"But that's where they go to... ah..."

"Go skinny dipping."

From the expression on Jacob's face, he was just a little bit embarrassed by what his mother knew about the swimming hole.

"Are you afraid to go there for some reason?" she continued.

"I'm not exactly afraid, it's just that..."

"Come down here and talk with me," Emily beckoned to her son.

Jacob turned and trudged back down the stairs. Emily directed him to the kitchen, sat him down then poured them both a glass of lemonade from a pitcher she kept in the refrigerator.

"What's the matter?" she asked her son.

"It's Jaclyn," he said.

He wasn't looking at his mother. She knew that it was serious.

"I think she wants me to make her pregnant."

He took a big swig of his lemonade.

"What makes you think that?" Emily asked.

"The other girl. She already is by her boyfriend, Mitch. When they came by to pick us up, Mitch told me that we'd be going up to the swimming place so that Jaclyn could have a baby, too. I felt uncomfortable and I really don't want to be a dad. Not yet, anyway."

Emily hid her emotions about Jacob's revelation. In her mind, she was ecstatic that her son had a moral compass – something she wasn't sure all teenagers had. He passed the test. He was tempted, but he passed the test.

"I'm glad to hear you say that, Jacob," she stated in a calm, positive manner. "I'm glad that you've paid back the trust your father and I have invested in you. I am going to call Jaclyn's mother. You understand why I need to do it, right?"

Jacob nodded his head and squirmed just a little. Emily excused him for the time being before calling the girl's mother. She gave the woman an account of the conversation she and Jacob had just had.

Jaclyn's mother expressed her gratitude for Emily's call. She asked Emily to bring Jacob over to her house, just so she could see for herself that Jacob wasn't with her daughter. A few minutes later, Emily was chatting with the other mother out in front of her house.

"Thank you, Mrs. Stevens," Jaclyn's mother said. "And thank you, Jacob for letting your mother know what was going on."

There was a short conversation between the women, ending in an invitation to attend Wednesday evening services. Emily's invitation was politely declined.

When Emily and Jacob got back to the house, Emily found herself getting increasingly anxious about Dan. She checked for messages on her cell phone at least twice before checking land lines for the church and their home.

"No news is good news," she tried to remind herself.

She started to call Dan several times, instead, trusting that if there was a problem, she would be contacted.

When Emily's cell phone rang with an unfamiliar number within the 304-area code, she hesitated before answering.

"Hello..."

"Emily Stevens?"

Emily confirmed her identity to the female voice on the other end.

"I'm Beasley. I work with the FBI."

"Why would a female agent try to call me?" thought Emily. Her mind filled with possible scenarios – none of them good.

"Your husband has been taken to the Tucker County Jail by the local sheriff."

"Your husband's in jail" were the four words Emily Stevens never expected to hear. She stood open-mouthed while a voice on the other end of the line brought her up to speed with the situation.

"He was hauled off by the sheriff just a few minutes ago," Beasley continued. "I've talked with him. James, I mean, agent Hamner's talked with him, too, and neither of us think he's done a thing."

"So, what's this about him being hauled off by the sheriff?" Emily asked.

"Agent Hamner took responsibility for your husband earlier today," Beasley explained. "The local sheriff here hates Hamner because he's black. The sheriff got a judge to issue a search and an arrest warrant based on a tip that there might be incendiary devices in your husband's car. They were just here, they found what they were looking for and the sheriff had your husband sent to the county seat."

"They found what?" Emily was confused.

"They found devices which could be used to start fires. I had a short conversation with agent Hamner before I called you; he's certain that your husband has nothing to do with either arson. The devices were most likely planted."

"Who would do such a thing," Emily mumbled.

"I have no idea. I will tell you this, though, I know a lawyer here local who can stall just long enough for us to get your husband out of the sheriff's hands, so we can find out who's responsible. We need your help, though."

"Do you need me to drive over?" Emily asked.

"No," Beasley said flat out. "If you were to show up here, the sheriff would have you thrown in jail for being an accessory. He's already breathing down pastor Gooding's neck, trying to implicate him as well. What I need from you are some sizes, so I can outfit your husband for some back-country camping."

"For what?"

"We're going to head for the hills, so to speak. Make him disappear for a while."

"Will he be safe?" Emily asked.

"Yes. My only concern is if you feel comfortable knowing your husband is alone in the company of another woman."

Beasley's stated concern caught Emily by surprise. She had the feeling that there was a sense of urgency in the request.

"How well do I really know the man I married?" she asked herself.

"Well enough to have had four children with him."

Her answer came immediately.

"Miss Beasley, I... I'm not quite certain," Emily almost told the FBI agent.

"He has earned your trust just as surely as you earned his."

"Okay," Emily mumbled her agreement.

"I need information; things like sizes so we can camp out in the wilderness for two to three days," Beasley stated.

After stammering for a short bit, Emily provided the agent with the information she needed. In return, Beasley revealed that she would take Dan into the back country at Dolly Sods to avoid re-arrest while other agents worked to find the person responsible for the church fire in Davis.

"Do I trust him alone with another woman?" Emily asked herself several times during the conversation.

"Would he trust me in a similar situation?"

Emily had her doubts about Dan… but she had doubts about herself at the same time.

It all came down to trust.

She took the call in the den. By the time the question of trust came up, she had wandered into the kitchen, where Jacob was rummaging through the refrigerator, looking for a late-afternoon snack.

"Knowing the right thing to do in a situation is a matter of example," she remembered Dan telling her repeatedly as their children were growing up.

"Jacob has just reflected the examples we've provided him," Emily thought. "I can trust my child. I can trust my husband. I can trust myself."

"Miss Beasley,"

"It's just Beasley."

"Please protect my husband the best way you know how," Emily told the agent. "When this is over, I want you to come and let me show my gratitude to you in person. May God be with you on the journey."

A feeling of peace descended on Emily Stevens when the call was concluded. Dan would be in good hands.

*****

A few hours later, closer to six, Peter called. He stated that he and Jacob were with the girls at their grandparents' and everyone wanted to know if there were plans for dinner. A quick conference later, a foray to Father Linguini's for pizza became the plan of the hour.

For some reason, Father Linguini's Most Excellent Pizza Parlor was busy on a Tuesday at dinner time. The Stevens family found a place to sit down. Grace and Hope became involved in an animated conversation while Peter and Jacob talked in hushed tones, trying to avoid their mother's ears. Jane Griswold sat down next to her daughter to even things out.

"What's the situation with Daniel?" Jane asked after their order was taken.

Emily brought her mother up to date with the latest news about her husband.

"You haven't heard from him yourself?" Jane asked.

"From what I understand, his cell phone got left behind when he was arrested. I'm sure he'll give me a call when he's able."

Emily wondered when Dan would be able but said nothing.

Mother and daughter went on for a few more minutes talking about much of nothing. Jane renewed her offer to take the children if Emily felt like going to meet Dan in West Virginia. Just before the food came to the table, Jane suddenly stopped talking.

"Try not to be too obvious, but someone just came in who looks like a dead ringer for that boy you had over to the house when you were Jacob's age," Jane whispered. "He's up at the counter now, picking up an order."

"What boy?" Emily asked.

"You know, the one you stole the kiss from in our backyard swimming pool."

Jacob overheard his grandmother and turned to try to see the man at the counter. Emily's face reddened at the memory.

"Jacob, you turn around right now," Emily hissed.

Peter got in on the action as well as Grace.

The man at the counter seemed to notice the attention. He turned away from the Stevens clan while he finished his transaction, leaving while deliberately avoiding eye contact.

"If that wasn't Eric Kovalo all grown up, then he sure was a dead ringer," Jane clucked shortly after the man left. The children were, by this time, staring out the window.

"And if it is, what about it," Emily shot back.

"Jacob, Grace, Peter, get away from that window," she commanded.

She was rattled; she knew that it was Eric Kovalo who left Father Linguini's in such a hurry.

"It's been at least twenty years since you brought him home that afternoon," Jane continued. "You could at least find out if it's really him…"

"Really who, Momma?" Grace asked while returning to her seat.

"The first boy your mother ever kissed…"

"MOTHER!!!" Emily hissed, hoping to avoid further questioning from her next to youngest child.

"You mean she kissed someone other than Daddy?" Grace asked her grandmother.

Jacob and Peter were back at the table, hanging on every word.

"Mother, Gracie, stop it!" Emily demanded.

The boys looked at each other and stifled their laughter. Hope searched from face to face attempting to figure out what was happening.

Emily took a deep breath and addressed Grace.

"Your grandmother thinks that that man is someone I knew when I was Jacob's age. It probably isn't, but if by some chance it is, it's the first time I've seen that man in years and years."

"Did you kiss him?"

Jacob and Peter hung on every word which was said, paying attention to the anticipated response to Grace's question.

"Yes, I kissed him," Emily sighed. "I had him over to my house just so I could kiss him."

"Did you have a baby?" Grace persisted.

"No, we did not," Emily stated slowly and carefully. "You know it takes more than a kiss to have a baby, Grace; Now would you please just drop the subject?"

She then pointed to her sons.

"And you two, leave it alone..."

"Emily..."

"Stay out of this, mother..."

"Emily, our meal is here."

"Oh," she said, finally standing down.

Inside of two minutes, everyone at the table was eating – everyone but Emily. She wondered who might have caught on to the exchange at the table. Most of the people in the pizzeria were from out of town, but there were one or two locals, including Tricia and Glenn Michaels. Tricia caught Emily's attention and motioned for her to join her in the bathroom.

She excused herself from her family and left the table.

"I take it that there's nothing new about Dan," Tricia queried Emily once the door to the restroom was closed.

"Not a whisper, other than he appears to be in the middle of a tug-of-war between the local sheriff and the FBI."

"Keep me posted, will you?" Tricia requested. "I'm working on something with Lizzie Elston, otherwise, I'd go with you to West Virginia to do a story about Dan."

Tricia turned the water on in the sink so that they wouldn't be heard outside of the bathroom.

"I presume you're thinking of driving over and seeing him," Tricia continued.

"Dan put me in charge of services until he's back," Emily replied. "With the kids and all, I'm afraid I can't."

"You know that there are people who would pick up the slack, right?"

"I know that, but I just… I don't know. What happens is in God's hands."

"And you're one of them… one of God's hands. At least in the way that Glenn and I feel. Make arrangements and just go, will you?"

"I can't, don't you see?"

Emily turned off the water and started to leave. Tricia lightly touched her arm to restrain her.

"Please…"

"It's in God's hands, like I just said," she reminded Tricia. "Dan may be a bit confused right now, but I don't think that he'd go so far as to start fires in churches. I'll wait things out for the next day or two, then see what happens. If I need to go, I'll go; you will be the first to know, okay?"

Tricia took her hand off Emily. "Promise?"

"Promise."

"What was the stir at your table a few moments ago?" Tricia asked just before Emily could leave.

"Nothing at all, really," Emily replied.

"It was an old boyfriend, right?"

"It's none of your business."

"He's an FBI agent assigned to the incidents here and in Davis."

"Who are you talking about," Emily almost sputtered.

"I'm talking about agent Kovalo – the fellow who just picked up a pizza. You know him, don't you?"

Emily blushed.

Tricia read Emily's face and continued.

"You knew him before. I can tell. So, what's the problem?"

"I suppose it's an issue of trust," Emily stated. "Jacob had a test earlier today and passed. I don't know if I would or not. And I'm also worried about Dan."

"You're worried that he's going to stray?" Tricia smiled. "I wouldn't. You had him from "hello". We've talked. He has you on a pedestal so high, no other woman could even hope to come close."

"I'm just afraid with what all has been going on lately that he might break," Emily confessed.

"He might bend, but he won't break," Tricia assured the pastor's wife.

"But he's having his doubts."

"On other matters. Not about you. Trust me."

Tricia gave Emily a short hug before leaving the bathroom.

Emily returned to the table with her mother and her children. She hardly touched the piece of pizza chosen for her by Grace. After they got back to the house, Jane pulled her daughter aside.
"That really was Eric Kovalo, wasn't it?" Jane enquired.

"I was told that it was," Emily admitted, "and I think he might have recognized me."

"It bothered you, didn't it?"

"Yeah, a little bit," Emily sighed. "I guess I'm more curious than anything, I mean, it was so long ago when his family moved away. I'd like to know what happened to him – how his life is going so far."

"You liked him, didn't you?" Jane pried.

"He did give me my first kiss," she winked.

"Do you think if you meet him again now that he'll sweep you off your feet and take you away from all of this?"

Emily looked around her. The idea of running away from her increasing responsibilities had a certain appeal. She looked again, took stock then realized that she was happy with what she had and what she found with Dan.

"If anything, I'd be afraid of breaking up whatever happiness he might have at this point in his life, mother," she rationalized. "After all, I chased him, remember?"

"Just like I chased your father until he caught me," Jane laughed.

The subject of Eric Kovalo went by the wayside. Jane eventually went back down the street to the small antiques shop she ran with Emily's father while Emily orchestrated a variety of activities to keep her children occupied for the rest of the evening.

Just after she got the children occupied, Emily's cell phone rang.

"Is this Mrs. Daniel Stevens?" a voice on the other end asked.

"Yes," she confirmed.

Something told her that there might be trouble connected with the call.

"Agent James Hamner," the voice informed her. "I'm calling to let you know that your husband and agent Beasley are safe for the time being. An agent in your area will be by shortly to bring you up to speed. Just so you know, God's at work, Mrs. Stevens. Your husband is in good hands."

Fifteen

An Epiphany of Trust

Emily recalled what Tricia Michael stated at Father Linguini's about him loving her and her alone from the word "hello". He was the stranger at the front door of her parents' house – the new assistant pastor her father wanted her to meet. She had just broken up, again, with Charlie Dill and was not particularly interested in spending an evening bored to tears while watching this new man squirm, while her father gave him the third degree. She told this stranger she wasn't interested at almost the instant she opened the door. In the second or two between saying what she felt she had to say and slamming the door in the assistant pastor's face, she saw her children.

Emily Griswold slumped down with her back to the door. She had been suddenly confronted with her future.

"When the time comes; when the right person comes along, the fact will hit you like a lightning bolt."

She recalled what her father told her less than four weeks earlier when she and Charlie called it quits again. She started panting – panicked.

Ken Griswold approached his daughter. She could tell by his smile that he knew what just happened. She didn't remember exactly what he said, but she did manage to recover her composure enough to open the door and apologize to the man who would soon be her husband.

During dinner, Emily could have sworn she was catching glimpses into the soul of Daniel Stevens. After dinner, they walked and talked late into the night. The next morning, she presented herself to the man she met just hours before. There would be no turning back for either of them. She had an epiphany about her future. There would be no turning back.

"Thank you, Mr. Hamner," she said to the agent on the phone. "If there's a way you can do it, send him my love."

"I'm praying for him too, ma'am."

She was still apprehensive.

Emily's apprehensions didn't end when she hung up the phone. She wasn't quite sure about Dan being out of touch in a place she didn't know in the company of a government agent. There were stories out there about sinister government plots to silence people who knew too much. Perhaps there was something Dan knew which threatened national security. Then again, he told her everything. He held nothing back and neither did she.

After thinking about it for a while, she concluded that she needed to trust Dan and trust the agents in West Virginia. Dan was in good hands.
*****

Just before bed-time, there was a knock on the Parsonage door. Emily hurried from the kitchen to find Gracie talking through the screen door to a man outside.

"Gracie, you need to get ready to go to bed," she told her child. Gracie turned and went on upstairs with Frank the Dog following closely behind. Emily turned her attention to her caller.

"Emily Griswold," the man stated. "Your daughter is charming. May I come in?"

It was Eric Kovalo. She stood, not knowing what to say or to do. Her heart was caught in her throat. He was just as handsome as she recalled him being when she was thirteen. Part of her wanted to drag him inside and make passionate love with him.

That wouldn't do. She had children, responsibilities, and a husband.

"I'm working with Bob Barada on your husband's case, Mrs. Stevens," Eric assured her, showing his badge. "It's a little late – at least twenty-two years, for a social call."

She went ahead and let him in, ushering him into the kitchen. She glanced upstairs to see her children and Frank watching to see what would happen next.

Emily let him inside and ushered him to the kitchen table.

"Let me cut to the chase," Kovalo said once they were inside and seated at her kitchen table. He pulled a drawing out of his top pocket and set it in front of her. "Have you ever seen this man?"

She studied the picture. There was something disturbingly familiar about the face which she couldn't quite put a finger on.

"Is this the drawing Miss Beasley told me about?" Emily asked.

Agent Kovalo nodded. "She has a reputation of being the best sketch artist the bureau has," he stated. "Your husband has already told us that this drawing is remarkably similar to someone he's seen in West Virginia these past couple of days."

She looked at the picture again. Again, she was sure that she'd seen the face.

"I… really have… I think I've seen this man, but, I'm not really certain when or where," she stammered.

"Well, there's a start. We think that this man may have a local connection. We don't know what it is yet, but we would appreciate it if you'd give us a call if you can think of who it might be."

He left the picture, got up and excused himself.

She got up and walked him to the door.

"You up and married a Marauder, huh?" Eric chuckled when they got to the door.

"Well, how about you? What have you done for yourself?" Emily asked.

"Married – divorced. Two girls, living with their mother up in Gahanna. I move around. I'm renting a room in Prentiss for the duration."

They chatted for a few minutes, exchanging a few details of each-others' lives before Eric called it an evening and left.

While she started to secure the front door, she heard a steady thump, thump, thump from the top of the stairs. She turned to see her three children and Frank the Dog watching her. She turned back to her task, stifling a laugh at the intense audience she had while saying goodnight to a former boyfriend.

Sixteen

Bubba

Rusty drove the cruiser back to the county seat fast enough to be safe, but too fast for Dan to be comfortable. The car tires squealed coming around blind corners. Dan thought about saying something about increasing the tire pressure on the tired, older Crown Victoria but figured that the enthusiastic deputy might take his comments out of context.

"Let them know that you're afraid and they'll most likely take more risks," Dan thought after flying through yet another blind corner at twice the suggested limit. He had received that advice prior to taking a helicopter ride between islands in Lake Erie.

They finally arrived in Parsons at a newer brick building housing the jail and the sheriff's office. Dan was led into a reception area where he was relieved of his personal items, booked and fingerprinted, all the while being watched by an elderly gentleman with a ring of white hair around a bald spot on top of his head. When the ordeal was over, and his mug shot taken, the older gentleman got up from his seat and approached.

"You're Pastor Stevens, I take it," the man stated, extending his hand. "I'm Bubba. Bubba Wolfe. My proper first name is Harlan. Beasley called and told me to come and meet you. If you let me, I'll be your lawyer."

Before Dan could respond, Rusty started to herd him toward the holding cells.

"Now look heah, Rusty," the old lawyer protested. "The man has a right to an attorney. You let us be for a few minutes in the conference room."

Dan began to ease away from the deputy. Rusty responded by pinning the pastor's arm behind his back.

"You're comin' with me," the deputy growled. "You try anything again, and I'll add resisting arrest to the charges against you."

"And I'll have you arrested for takin' away this man's rights!" Bubba exclaimed. "Now you let that man go and leave him to me!"

Rusty reluctantly relented. He released Dan and pointed him toward a small room just off the hallway. Dan joined the lawyer, went into the room with a pair of metal chairs and a heavy wooden table.

"You sit over here with your back to the window," Bubba instructed the pastor. "That way they can't read your lips. Deputy Larson at the front desk is partially deaf and he knows how."

Dan sat down in the chair as Bubba instructed.

"Beasley told me that you might need my help," the lawyer began. "She's already filled me in on some of the details. What I need to know is why the sheriff's men found fire starters in the trunk of your car."

"I suppose I do need help," Dan told him. "As far as the incendiary devices found in the trunk of my car, I have no earthly idea how they got there. The car belongs to my wife, anyway, and I think I might have noticed if there was anything in the trunk other than the suitcases I brought on the trip."

"Beasley told me that the devices were under the trunk in the spare tire well."

"That would explain why I didn't see them."

Dan's mind started racing. He wondered if maybe Emily had something to do with the fire in Magnolia. He quickly discarded the notion.

"I'm going to take your word that you knew nothing about the extra baggage in your trunk," Bubba Wolfe declared. "Beasley told me that you might have seen someone suspicious earlier today."

Dan was amazed that Bubba changed the subject so quickly.

"Was it someone you've seen before?" the elderly lawyer asked.

"Forget that."

The lawyer changed course yet again.

"We need to get you out of here before the sheriff – "

Bubba cut his musings short. Dan heard the click of the door behind him.

"Well, hello Bubba..." Dan recognized the sheriff's voice. "I ain't had the chance to talk to my prisoner yet, and here you are, prepping him so's he can get off Scot-free. We know he done it and we got the evidence – so you run along now, y'hear?"

Bubba stood up. Dan turned to watch him as he stood toe to toe with the sheriff. Bubba was a good three inches shorter than the lawman, but it became apparent that Bubba was the bigger man.

"All you have are anonymous tips, circumstance and too much time watching cop and lawyer shows," Bubba scolded the lawman. "You know damn good and well that the recent church arsons are under investigation as a federal crime. You're out of your jurisdiction, George and you know that, too."

Sheriff George Pinkerman was getting red in the face.

"It's because of Agent Hamner, isn't it, George?"

"That ignorant nigger don't know nothin'," the sheriff growled. "We got his arsonist for him, and by God, I'm gonna see that I get the credit, not him!"

Sheriff Pinkerman tried to reach around Bubba to drag Dan out of the conference room. Bubba blocked him.

"You'll do no such thing!" Bubba told the sheriff. "Agent James Hamner is on his way here right now, and if you use the n-word one more time at least in my presence, I'll see to it that you'll need a plumber to help you swallow your lunch!"

The sheriff stepped back. Dan surmised that Bubba and the sheriff had tangled on more than one occasion.

"Your boy better be here inside of fifteen minutes." Sheriff Pinkerman spat on the floor at Bubba's feet. "Otherwise, I'm personally taking your client to the cell block."

The sheriff stormed back out, slamming the conference room door behind him.

"From the sounds of it, he has a giant-sized chip on his shoulder," Dan remarked.

"More like a forest," Bubba chuckled. "All the more reason to get you out of here and out of sight as soon as possible."

"Would agent Hamner be coming?" Dan asked.

"I sure as hell hope so. I told Beasley to send him here. Hopefully she'll be able to get a hold of him. I don't think there'll be a problem. I've known Hamner for a while. Good man. I've been trying to convince him to settle here in Tucker County and run for sheriff instead of that jerk."

"Wouldn't the local folk have something to say about it?" Dan asked. "I mean, how long has sheriff Pinkerman been in office?"

"He's been in for the better part of a dozen years," Bubba informed him. "No one's run against him in the past couple of elections... or should I say that no one has had the guts to run against him in the past couple of elections."

"I take it he gets all the votes, then."

"Hardly anyone voted for him. He only got two-hundred seventy-seven votes last election, out of over fifteen-hundred cast. Don't get me wrong. He's not a dirty cop – in fact he's a really good cop, but he has a propensity for pissing off the wrong people at the wrong time."

"Like dropping that n-bomb, right?"

Bubba smiled. "There are still lots of folks here who think it's okay to call a man an n-word. James lets it roll off his back – tells me he thinks it's okay, but I know deep down it hurts him."

"We're all equal in the sight of the Lord," Dan said quietly.

"Glad you said that," Bubba replied. "Now I know for sure that I can trust you. Now, before James gets here, tell me, why are you in Tucker County, and tell me what you can about this mystery man you think you saw."

Dan told the lawyer about his trip from Magnolia, including why he made it. He established that he was a guest and that he knew nothing about the items found in his trunk.

"I do recall, at least I think I recall someone coming up or going down the drive to the cabin on Sunday night," Dan pointed out. "It might mean something, or it might mean nothing. I have no idea."

"You have an idea whether it was a man or a woman you heard?"

"I couldn't tell you," Dan said after pondering for a moment or two.

"Maybe we'll have to go back up to your cabin and have a look," Bubba said.

"Maybe the best thing for me to do is to go up to the cabin, gather whatever hasn't been rifled through and go home," Dan sighed.

"The sheriff would be on you in a New York minute. If I wasn't involved, he'd find a way to have you shot while trying to escape."

"He wouldn't do that would he?"

"Don't bet that he wouldn't."

Bubba paced back and forth in the conference room while Dan watched him, wondering what would happen next.

Snippets of polite conversation passed back and forth between the men for a little over an hour. Dan and Bubba discovered that they both had a love for fast cars and raising hell in their youth.

"My daddy got tired of bailing me out of trouble all the time," Bubba confessed. "Told me that I should become a lawyer. That was before I learned that a lawyer defending himself has a fool for a client."

"I wonder if the same rule applies to pastors?" Dan postulated. "I feel as if maybe being a pastor is driving me away from God."

"You're busy with your flock, I take it," Bubba winked. "You take on too much and you're sure to burn out sooner or later."

Bubba paused. "Poor choice of words, son. I apologize."

"It's okay," Dan assured the lawyer. "Pastors are known to have a high burnout rate – and some of them do take drastic measures when they're under pressure. Years ago, we had a preacher go berserk in my hometown; he killed his wife and his kids, set fire to his church and committed suicide right in front of my best friend."

"Ouch," Bubba winced. "Sounds like that preacher was a bubble or two off plumb."

"That was an extreme case. I don't think I'm that far along, yet, but I feel as if I may be headed in that direction."

Sheriff Pinkerman dropped by for the fifth time since Dan and Bubba went into the conference room. Each time, he declared that his patience was wearing thin and that he wanted to put Dan in a holding cell. Each time the sheriff made his wishes known, Bubba insisted that he needed more time to debrief his client. This time, he came in armed with a shotgun. He wasn't going to be denied.

"You've had enough talk, preacher. You're coming with me," Sheriff Pinkerman insisted.

"Help's on the way," Bubba confided. "In the meantime, let the sheriff have his way."

Dan reluctantly followed the sheriff out of the room. He was led down a narrow corridor to a steel door guarded by someone who was clearly bored by his job guarding the door. The man got up and handed Dan a parcel.

"Strip, then put these on," the sheriff instructed.

129

Inside the parcel was an orange jumpsuit and a pair of slippers for his feet.

"No underwear?" Dan asked.

"You ain't gonna be wearin' any, preacher. Now, hurry up. I ain't got time for your nonsense."

Dan reluctantly peeled out of what he was wearing, aware that every move he made was being carefully watched by a pair of men who obviously felt he was guilty of whatever it was they might be accused of doing. He felt shame at being naked, alone and vulnerable.

He quickly donned the jumpsuit after being carefully inspected by the men guarding him. Trust was absent in this place.

He was alone. Emily, Jacob, Peter, Grace and Hope were fading from his memory.

He was about to take his first step into the belly of a beast where even God was reluctant to tread.

Seventeen

In Awe of the Universe

A commotion on the other end of the hallway became the pinch which helped Dan Stevens wake up from what was fast becoming a nightmare.

"Sheriff, that better be my prisoner you have there!"

James Hamner's voice boomed down the hallway. Dan's heart started beating again.

"Goddamned nigger," Sheriff Pinkerman hissed under his breath.

"If that's Daniel Stevens, he needs to come with me to that new federal lockup in Fairmont. He's too damn dangerous for you in this rinky-dink outfit, Pinkerman."

James reached the trio at the steel door, flashed his badge and took hold of Dan's arm.

"But I didn't..." Dan started to defend himself.

"You keep quiet," James ordered. "I don't want to hear a word out of you. Are those the prisoner's belongings, sheriff?"

The sheriff spit in the container where just minutes ago Dan was instructed to put his clothes. Agent Hamner let go of Dan, grabbed hold of the sheriff and pulled him right up to his face.

"I've had all I can stand out of you, sheriff," James growled. "I have a good mind to take you into custody for tampering with evidence. One more peep out of you and I'll have a federal marshal here to lock you up for hampering my investigation. Have I made myself clear?"

The sheriff made a small nodding motion. The G-man pushed him away.

"You," he commanded the person guarding the door, "take this man's belongings and follow me out to my car."

James herded Dan and the unfortunate door ward out of the hallway, through the booking area and outside to a waiting car. He was quite literally stuffed into the back seat and told not to move while his belongings went into the trunk. James then dismissed the deputy and drove Dan away from the sheriff's office.

"I thought you were my friend," Dan said once they were clear of the building. "What's this about taking me to a federal lock-up?"

"There is no federal lock-up. I'm getting you away from that idiot sheriff. If you were in real trouble with me, I'd have you in handcuffs right now. Fasten your seat belt."

Dan suddenly came to the realization that aside from being in the back seat of a government issued car and wearing an orange jumpsuit, he was a free man.

"It'll probably take him about fifteen minutes to figure out that he's been bamboozled. By that time, we'll have you tucked out of the way where he can't find you."

"How? Where?" Dan asked.

"Practically right under his nose," James told him. "Beasley's up at your cabin waiting to take you up on the ridge. We've got what I hope is a good, solid lead on our perpetrator and we hope to get him under lock and key within forty-eight hours."

Dan's curiosity was satisfied for the moment. He let down his guard for the time being while he was driven back to the cabin where his troubles began earlier in the day.

Beasley was there to meet them. She was sitting on the front porch, guarding a pair of backpacks. There was little time for formalities. James recovered Dan's clothes from the trunk and told him to put them on. Dan stripped out of the jump suit and put on his regular clothes while Beasley and James loaded the backpacks into the back of his car.

"You may want to wear these instead of your regular shoes," Beasley suggested, handing him a pair of hiking shoes. "I talked with your wife and told her what was going on. She gave me your sizes and I pulled together some things you'll need for our trek."

"I need to talk with her," Dan told Beasley. "Could I use your phone?"

"It would be better if you didn't," she informed him. "She knows that you're safe and she knows that we are working to keep you that way."

"Why can't I talk with her?"

"We don't have the cell coverage out here, and we don't have the time to use a land line," Beasley explained.

"You two quit jabbering," James demanded. "Let's get in this car and let's get out of here!"

In less than a minute, they were roaring south on the state highway. They went out of the valley then headed out a rural lane at a quick, yet safe pace. At what seemed to be the end of a road, they crossed a low bridge over a rocky creek. The road became gravel and wound uphill through a forest for what seemed to Dan to be forever.

While they ascended, Beasley pulled out a map to study.

"How much further?" James asked once they appeared to emerge out of the woods.

"About three miles," Beasley answered, folding the map. "We should have enough light to make it a mile off the road to a place where we can camp for the night."

"We're camping?" Dan asked.

"Sorry, there are no cabins up here," Beasley told him. "This is a wilderness area. Dolly Sods. We'll be safe here while sheriff numb nuts tries to figure out where you are on the trail between Davis and the resort."

"Why would he be looking there?"

"We left him some clues… your jumpsuit, my car…" Beasley shot Dan a devilish grin. "Pastor Gooding, if asked, will tell the sheriff he saw us going up to the cabin, so he makes the logical leap and sends his posse up on the trail between the resort and Blackwater."

"Here?" James asked, slowing down the car.

"About half a mile further. There's a cutout. You'll see it," Beasley replied.

"The three of us, right?"

Dan saw James' face twisted up in the rear-view mirror.

"Just you two," James said. "I need to go back down the mountain to keep an eye on things."

"Over there, James!"

Beasley pointed out a spot where James could pull off the side of the road to allow passengers access to a trail head. James pulled to the side and got out, so he could help Dan and Beasley unload the camping supplies in the trunk. In less than three minutes, a pair of backpacks and a duffle were on the ground. Beasley and Dan watched James drive back down the gravel road in the same direction from which they came.

"Well, put on your pack and let's go," Beasley announced. "We're going about a mile west then a little north before we get to a place to camp."

She picked up one of the packs, slinging it on her back. It was obvious to Dan that she had done this before. He puzzled over the arrangement before picking up the other pack. In his trial lift, he was amazed that the pack wasn't as heavy as he might have guessed. Beasley gave him some instruction before helping him don the load. Making sure that her charge was comfortable, she picked up the duffle then headed away from the road using a lightly used path.

"When do we stop?" he asked after they had hiked for about ten minutes.

"When we get there."

"Are there facilities on the way?"

"No. We're packing everything we need in on our backs."

"I meant, is there a bathroom?"

"I know what you meant. If you must stop and pee, stop and pee wherever you want. I'll wait."

"I don't have to pee."

Beasley stopped.

"If you need to take a crap… wait a moment."

She reached around and took a folding spade from the outside of her backpack.

"Here," she said, handing him the spade. "What you do is dig a small hole with this. Squat and do your business then cover the hole back up. There are some wipes to clean yourself with in your backpack."

The idea of defecating in the open held little appeal to Dan, besides, he didn't really need to go then. He thanked Beasley for the instruction then returned her spade.

"Just a little advice when the time comes," Beasley mentioned when they were back on their way, "you need to be careful where you dig. This whole area was part of a firing range back during the war. There's still pieces of unexploded ordnance out there."

"You're kidding."

"No, I'm not. There are signs by the side of the road warning people."

"Are the old shells still being found?"

"Every once in a great while, yeah. Mostly harmless, but they're still out there."

Dan made a mental note to stay close to Beasley and not wander off the trail. An hour after they left the gravel road, they came on a relatively flat and open spot on the trail. It was obvious by the presence of a fire ring that this had been a stopping point for other campers.

"We should be good here for the night," Beasley announced. "If you need it, there's a pit about a hundred-fifty foot that way which is usable; a makeshift latrine if you will."

Dan thanked her, found the wipes then went to do his business. When he returned, Beasley had already set up a small dome tent and was in the process of gathering pieces of wood to start a fire.

"Where do I set up my tent?" Dan asked when he had her attention.

"We're sharing this one," Beasley told him. "It's a little cozy, but we'll manage."

"I don't know if I can trust you."

"I think it's more of a case of you may not know if you can trust yourself," she pointed out. "I can appear to be an easy target – considering that your wife is two hundred miles away and bearing the battle scars of having children. I'd be tempted, too, if I were you."

"This is an awkward situation."

"It's only as awkward as you care to make it Mr. Stevens."

Beasley excused herself and headed toward the pit while Dan wished that he had his cell phone, so he could call Emily. He sat down on one of the rocks in the fire ring and started to explore what items he had in his pack. Near the top, he found that Beasley had packed his Bible.

"You told me that you were Wiccan when we met earlier today," Dan commented when she returned. "I see that you packed my Bible. Why?"

"Because I respect your beliefs," she told him. "You respected me when I told you what I believed; I thought I would reciprocate."

"The golden rule," he smiled.

"All religions I know of practice it in some form," Beasley responded, sitting down on a rock opposite Dan. "The same goes for everything in the world around us. Take our little hike, for example. We tread carefully and respect the environment, so the environment doesn't bother us in return. Make a misstep and there are any number of ways you can end up having a bad day.

"By the way," she added, "I called your wife while you were in town and let her in on our plans for you. Gave her a full disclosure. She seems to be okay with this arrangement."

"Really?" he asked. "What about you? What about your significant other? What do you know about me?"

"James had you vetted before he even took you to the burned-out church, for one," Beasley started. "We know more about you than you might even know about you. At first, I suggested you staying with him in his apartment up in Maryland. He suggested this trip – said something about a trip in the wilderness being helpful to where you were in your life. As far as having a significant other, I have no significant other and I really don't anticipate ever having one. If I did, what I do on my job is my business alone."

"This is just a job for you?"

"Yes and no. Yes, this is my job, but at the same time, I love coming up here. You'll see why after it gets dark."

Beasley proceeded to go through her pack, unloading items she thought would be helpful, including left-over pizza from earlier in the day.

138

She enlisted Dan's help in building and lighting a small fire, all the while guiding the conversation winding around his personal life.

"Your boys sound like they can be a handful," she remarked after Dan told her about Jacob and Peter.

"Jacob's to the point in life where he's starting to chase girls," Dan laughed.

"You were pretty shy at that point of your life, as I understand it."

Dan blushed a little.

Beasley embarrassed him more, relating what she had found out about Dan's dating life before he met Emily.

"She's lucky, you know," Beasley remarked.

"I'm the lucky one," he replied. "You know, until I met her, I never thought that there was such a thing as love at first sight."

By this point in their conversation, the sun had gone beyond the horizon – the lingering twilight painted in various hues of orange and violet. Stars started to come out to start their nightly travels through the skies. The fire which warmed their supper and warmed their souls had died down to the point where it seemed pointless to continue fueling the blaze.

"You said something about not having a significant other," Dan probed. "Do you think you'll ever find someone to share your life with?"

"You sound like a matchmaker," Beasley said with a twinkle in her voice. "I'm already in love with the world around me. I feel complete... like you do with Emily."

"I can respect that," Dan told her after thinking for a few moments.

She got up and bade him good night.

He stayed outside of the tent for the better part of an hour, wondering if it was okay for him to go inside and crawl in his sleeping bag. At the same time, he marveled in awe of the universe unfolding around him.

A different set of night noises played out around him. He almost fell asleep a couple of times before deciding it was time to go inside. After saying a short prayer for Emily and his children, he slipped into the tent, crawled over the sleeping woman inside and wrapped himself into his sleeping bag.

Eighteen

Answered Prayers

Emily spent a restless night. She woke up several times to reach over to her missing husband, just to feel his body next to hers. She finally gave up at half past four in the morning and went downstairs, hoping that he had somehow escaped and made it back home.

She stepped out onto the back patio to face east. Daniel was out there somewhere, probably wanting her as much as she wanted him. Standing, she marveled at the heavens above her. Patterns in the stars spoke of the existence of a greater power – God – and of the vastness of the universe surrounding her.

Emily Stevens was alone; yet surrounded by love.

Except for the sounds of the occasional car on the highway going around Magnolia, it was quiet.

"Mom..."

Peter's voice broke the silence. The boy joined his mother.

"Is Dad okay?"

"He's fine, I know it."

Peter sidled up to his mother and held her hand. They were silent for a while. The door behind them opened. Gracie joined them.

Then Jacob, finally Hope.

Emily took in deep breaths of the pre-dawn air, feeling the love of her family – feeling the love of God.

"We'll make it through this," she assured her children. "We will not be abandoned. Your father will come home. Our church will be rebuilt."

The children hugged their mother, believing every word she said, although she had difficulty believing it herself.

By five, the children were back in bed asleep. Emily lay in her lonely bed, still wide awake, worried about how the day would unfold.

She didn't have long to wait.

Almost instantly it was six. By six thirty, she was dressed in running shorts and a sports bra, wearing a pair of running shoes. Chloe Thompson was at her front door. Both ran out in the country, out Hemry Hollow Road. Emily had to be coaxed by the younger woman to push herself just a little harder to go a little faster around the five-mile loop they usually ran.

By the time they returned at seven, the children were starting to stir again. Jacob was already up at the breakfast table plugging away at some computer game Emily pretended to understand. She was okay with the gaming. It kept him out of the troubles some of his peers were experiencing. Hope sat next to him, sporting a clean pull-up and eating a bowl of cereal obviously served by her older brother.

Frank the Dog came bounding down the stairs followed closely by Grace and Peter. Instantly the kitchen became a mad house with a flurry of activity. The two middle children flitted in different directions to get their own breakfasts, each ignoring their siblings, favoring their own needs instead. Emily let Frank out the back door. She and Chloe took some hydration from the refrigerator then went out to sit on the patio while the family dog patrolled the perimeter to ensure their safety.

"Motherhood seems to suit you," Chloe remarked once they settled away from the din of the kitchen. "I don't know if I'll ever be able to handle having children of my own."

"The first one's the hardest, but once you get used to having them around, you'd be amazed at how easily you can adjust," Emily told her. "Sometimes you'll have to put other portions of your life on hold, but eventually you'll realize that raising children is quite rewarding as anything you'll ever do."

"It helps that you have a supportive husband," Chloe observed.

"My understanding is that Christopher is just as supportive," Emily pointed out. "When the time comes to make the commitment, he'll be there for you. Trust me."

Emily saw the signs. Chloe was pregnant. She didn't know it yet, but Emily already knew.

Chloe took a long pull at her water as her way to show that she was shifting gears in the conversation.

"What's Dan's status this morning? Have you heard from him?"

"Not directly, no," Emily sighed. "I've been in contact with a pair of agents in West Virginia. They have Dan hiding out somewhere out of the reach of the county sheriff. The sheriff thinks that Dan's the arsonist, at least in the Davis case. The FBI thinks otherwise. Right now, he's like a ping-pong ball between the sheriff and the feds."

"You know that everyone will be asking about him at tonight's service," Chloe stated.

"I know, and I dread having to go through with it – but I have to. It's expected."

Chloe offered to help in any way she could before heading home to change before going to work. Emily agreed to have lunch with her at Zeke's Café to discuss the situation in more detail. In the meantime, she had a houseful of children to contend with. Jacob and Peter could take care of themselves, but Emily took care to remind them that they had limits. Grace volunteered to watch after Hope if they could go to the playground in the park. It was suggested that the pair go to see their grandmother; perhaps they could find what they needed to have High Tea on their grandmother's back porch.

Arrangements were made, and within half an hour Emily was alone. She secreted herself into Dan's home study to develop an action plan for the rest of her day.

She started with a prayer.

It was answered with a phone call.

Emily's mother was on the other end.

"Do you think that Hope may be ready for a week away from both of her parents?" Mrs. Griswold asked. "Your father and I are thinking of heading up to Kelly's Island for a while and thought it might not be a bad idea to take the children with us."

For some reason, the idea sounded perfect to Emily. She needed the time to decompress, if nothing else.

"When would you be leaving?" she asked.

"As soon as we can make the arrangements," Mrs. Griswold answered. "After services tonight at the earliest."

"That soon?" Emily queried.

Wheels in her head started to turn. There were a few loose-ends which needed to be taken care of before Dan returned. He would return. Tired as she was, she was certain that he would return.

"If you go ahead and make the arrangements, I'd appreciate it," Emily continued. "If you leave tonight, I'll need you to come and help pack. I still have a sermon to write and a number of other chores to tend to."

Jane Griswold agreed, telling Emily that she would be back later with details and the girls.

Now it was Emily and a blank piece of paper, ready to accept the sermon she would be preaching that evening.

The blank piece of paper sat there, staring her in the face. It mocked her. She got up from the desk to go into the kitchen to get a glass of lemonade. The fact that there wasn't any already made sent her to the freezer to see if she had any frozen lemonade mix. None there, either, so she went upstairs to put on something more amenable for a trip to the grocery store.

While she changed, she pulled out a different piece of paper and started a grocery list.

"Why are grocery lists so easy and sermons are so hard?" she asked the empty room.

She took the list downstairs and placed the list next to the blank piece of paper hoping that somehow the list would migrate into the words she needed for her sermon.

No such luck.

Her mind wandered back to Dan, then to Eric Kovalo. Was it coincidence or was it by purpose that he would show up at her door at nearly ten o'clock the night before? She shook off the thought, picked up her list and headed to Mulligan's.

Steve Mulligan himself greeted her while she was in line waiting to check out.

"Do you have your talk ready for tonight," he asked once the pleasantries were out of the way.

"I'm stalling," she confessed. "I still have a blank piece of paper at the house."

"Would you rather I give the talk?" he asked.

She hoped that he would offer. Emily wanted to say yes immediately, but she didn't want to seem overly anxious.

"If I still have a blank piece of paper by noon, I'll let you know," she told him.

Emily returned home, put up what she had purchased at the market, fidgeted for a few minutes and then went back into the study where she hoped that the blank piece of paper would have at least a few words on it to inspire her to write more.

There was no such miracle.

She finally relented and called to ask Steve Mulligan to deliver the sermon that evening. He agreed, affirming that she had too much on her plate at that time.

With the item of the sermon off the plate, Emily enjoyed her lunch with Chloe at Zeke's Café.

"Can I share something with you, and can you keep it secret for a short while?" Chloe asked Emily almost in a whisper.

"Sure."

"I think I'm pregnant," Chloe confided.

"I thought you might be," Emily smiled. "Have you confirmed it, yet?"

"Not yet. I'm driving up to Prentiss to see a doctor this afternoon. I was hoping you'd come with me."

"I'll be happy to," she agreed. "Have you taken a home test?"

"No," Chloe answered. "I want to surprise Christopher. Asking him to bring home a test kit would tip him off prematurely."

Emily laughed. Chloe's husband, Christopher Michaels, ran Village Pharmacy.

"If you want, I can get you a kit," she offered. "That way, you won't be wasting a visit to the clinic."

"I already have my visit scheduled," Chloe said to decline Emily's offer to purchase a pregnancy test. "I've prayed, and I've made up my mind that I want to be a mother. It's time."

Emily gave Chloe a hug. "You'll make a fine mother," she told Chloe. "I'll be happy to come with you and share your joy."

Chloe thanked her before going on her way. Going with Chloe to the county clinic was another item on Emily's plate, but one she gladly accepted.

Dan sensed that he was chilly. His first thought was to snuggle just a little closer to Emily to rob her of some of her body heat.

He realized that he wasn't in his bedroom. He was still fully clothed and stuffed in the sleeping bag he crawled into just a few hours earlier.

"Beasley," he said softly. Surely Beasley was in the sleeping bag next to his.

The other sleeping bag was empty.

Daniel Lee Stevens came to the realization that he was a fugitive from the law, trapped in the wilderness, led there by a woman connected with the FBI.

"I know people who would have a field day with this scenario," he thought.

The chill was taken over by the need to pee. Dan wiggled out of the sleeping bag then maneuvered around to put on the pair of hiking shoes he left at the door of the tent. When he finally emerged, he was greeted by a re-kindled fire. Beasley was on the other side of the fire, turned away from him facing the gathering light from the soon to be rising sun. Her arms were outstretched as if she were poised to gather all the sunlight once it peeked its way past the line of trees on the edge of the clearing.

Despite the chill, Beasley stood in the gathering light as naked as the day she was born.

"When you've finished your business, I've made some coffee," she said, not moving from where she stood. "We need to have a talk before we pack up and move along."

Dan said nothing. He went an appropriate distance from the encampment, voided his bladder then returned.

Beasley hadn't moved.

He averted his eyes while coughing to attract her attention.

"Is there a problem?" Beasley responded.

"No problem, it's just that I'm uncomfortable with you standing there like that," Dan admitted.

"Like facing where the sun will be coming up? Are you afraid I'm going to go blind by looking into it?"

"I'm uncomfortable that my wife will find out."

"About what?"

"About you standing naked in front of me," Dan was finally able to spit out.

Beasley laughed and turned. She brushed past him then fished out her back pack from the tent. Declaring Dan to be silly, she extracted a shirt and a pair of hiking shorts, put them on then proceeded to work on serving the coffee.

"You're a killjoy, you know that?" Beasley commented after both had started sipping their coffee. "I was celebrating my oneness with the world around me when you came out. If I interrupted your prayer time, wouldn't you be upset?"

"You're considering standing naked in the middle of nowhere prayer time?"

Dan stopped himself. She stayed quiet, looking at him, knowing that he'd reached an epiphany.

"Do you genuflect when you approach an altar?" She eventually asked. "Do you face Mecca and drop to your knees when it's time for prayer? Do you put on a shawl and a skull cap to praise God? Do you sprinkle, or do you immerse when you baptize someone? Do you sing acapella or does your church use musical instruments?"

Dan acknowledged her point while she peppered him with questions.

"You win," he finally admitted. "You told me yesterday that you were Wiccan. I should have expected and respected your space."

"Not only that, I'm a witch!" A mischievous grin crossed her face. "And if you don't watch it, I'll turn you into a newt!"

They had a hearty, bonding laugh.

Dan got the message and apologized. Working together over the next hour, they had breakfast then broke camp. Beasley instructed him on several finer points while they were packing up.

"The plan for today is to go back the way we came," she told him while they were hoisting their packs onto their backs. "Hopefully we can make it to the Red Creek campground at the next trailhead without being spotted by the sheriff."

"How long will it take us to get there?" he asked.

"Judging from the pace we went yesterday; I anticipate the hike to take us about three hours provided there are no complications. We'll camp overnight again then spend the next two days along the Blackbird Knob Trail before getting picked up at the trail head at Canaan Valley. By that time James should have the case wrapped up and you'll be going home."

Beasley started back up the path without saying another word. Dan thought it best to just follow her for the time being, but at the same time, he was getting a little anxious about what could happen in the next few days. Several times on their march to the road, Dan almost tried to say something to his escort, but never got around to it. Each time he started to open his mouth, Beasley would bring him to a halt and point out a feature along their path. There were birds, small animals and evidence of the animals' passing. At one point, she called his attention to a spider's web along the path. The web was heavy with dew, glistening in the morning sunlight. He stopped and took notice of the regularity of the web along with the intricacy of the trap.

"God's hands can be seen in the smallest of things and in the largest of things," he recalled a sermon he'd given not long after Hope was born. "Look around you. Take the time to just look, listen and observe."

He wished at times that he'd have followed his own advice. In the months after the birth of his youngest daughter, Dan's plate was full. After helping Emily through her post-partum blues, he essentially became both mother and father to his children. She spent much of her time attending classes while he juggled his time between the church and the needs of his children. He had precious little time, until now, to literally stop and smell the roses.

Close to the end of the first stage of the day's journey, Beasley stopped Dan, took off her pack and told him to stay where he was until she scouted ahead.

He resisted asking why, knowing that if Hope was with them, she'd ask the same question.

Beasley stalked off.

A short time later, she returned.

"The road is thirty yards ahead," she reported. "I see signs of activity in both directions. We need to be quick. We need to be ready to hide in an instant."

"What's the matter?" Dan queried.

"There's a sheriff's cruiser parked a quarter mile down the road. Fortunately, he's pointed in the other direction. Unfortunately, he appears to be stopping passersby – most likely giving them warnings about us."

"Should we go back to the campsite?"

"No," she stated quite clearly. "My guess is that the sheriff's sent someone to flush us out from the other end of the trail. Deputy Hill knows the area and he knows about the site. I left signs which I hope will throw him off our trail, but it will only be a matter of time before he figures out the ruse and heads this way."

"How much time do you think we have?"

"Minutes or hours. He has the advantage of having a radio and not having a pack."

"What do we do?"

"We need to head north along the road," she told him. "For at least the first mile, we need to stick to the side to keep our exposure to a minimum. After that, we need to move as quickly as possible to the campground. Hopefully there'll be safe-haven available."

Beasley put her pack back on then led Dan to the roadway. She motioned him to be quiet. He heard the chatter of a police radio coming from the direction opposite that which they were going to take. Beasley directed his attention to the car, partially hidden by a rise in the road. The cruiser's door opened. Dan saw a deputy get out, look up and down the road, and then disappear.

"Now's our chance," Beasley whispered, while pulling Dan along the side of the road.

They put some distance between themselves and the trail head, jogging as best as they could along the rim of the road. After several minutes spent at a frantic pace, Beasley urged Dan onwards while she reconnoitered.

"Nature's call," she told him when she caught back up. "Someone had breakfast tacos and coffee before he came up here. He moved the car to cover the trail head, by the way. We got out just in time."

They continued their journey, mostly in silence for the next hour. Occasionally, Beasley beckoned Dan to head for cover on the side of the road. The occasional car would pass then they were back on their way again.

A large rooster-tail of dust coming from behind when they were roughly three miles away from the trail head sent Dan and Beasley off to the side of the road just a little further than had been before. She slipped out of her pack and urged Dan to do the same. In less than a minute, a pair of sheriff's cruisers were zipping along the dirt road as fast as they dared to go.

"Hill must have made it to the other end," she murmured.

Dan started to get up to put his backpack on after the cruisers passed. Beasley pulled him back down into their hiding spot.

"They'll be back in this direction in less than fifteen minutes," she told him. "It's best if we just stay put for the time being."

He stayed hidden. To keep his mind off his predicament, he looked up and watched as the clouds skittered by.

The sheriff's cruisers made another pass, then another.

"How much longer are we going to stay here?" Dan asked after the third pass.

"We may be stuck here for another hour or more," she informed him. "The sheriff suspects we're out here somewhere and that somehow we're going to slip up and show our hand."

Dan wasn't too happy at the prospect of staying in one place for an extended period. Beasley sensed his discomfort and initiated a conversation.

"Tell me about your children," she began. "Emily told me that you had four of them."

Dan took a deep breath. Beasley's tone of voice told him that he could trust her as much now as she must have trusted him earlier.

"Jacob's the oldest. He's fourteen and he's noticing girls. Peter is two years younger and he seems to be following in his brother's footsteps... regarding girls, that is. Gracie is nine. She's a real hoot. Thinks she's in charge. And then there's Hope. She's two and already talking. Her favorite word these days is "why"."

"A friend of mine has a three-year old," Beasley revealed. "That seems to be his favorite question, too."

"Do you eventually want children of your own?" Dan asked.

"No," she told him. "I'm not sure that I even want to have a life partner. Family, even just two people, is a commitment – one I'm not sure I'd want to take on."

"Family does have its rewards," he pointed out.

"And it has its pitfalls, too. I am a child of divorce, Dan. My parents broke up just after I left high school. As it turns out, my father didn't care for my mother. He only stuck around because he felt he had to."

"I take it that he impregnated your mother with you?"

Beasley nodded. "I'm an only child. My parents never had relations after I was born... with each other, that is. My father kept a woman over in Petersburg, or so I've been told. Mother broke up at least three other marriages by her fooling around. She confessed to me to having had an abortion because of one of them. She never said anything to my father, but I think he knew."

"Do you have a love life?" he asked.

"I've never known a man, in the Biblical sense, that is. I came close once. That deputy back at the roadblock, the one who went and evacuated himself a while back, I almost did the deed with him. He complained about the size of my breasts. I decided that I didn't need the hassle. I walked out on him and never looked back."

"Good for you," Dan praised her. "You respected yourself. It's something God would want you to do."

"I thought your Bible said something about a woman having to submit to a man," Beasley stated.

"All the Bible really says is to love God and love your neighbor. As a Jewish friend of mine would say, all the rest is commentary."

Beasley smiled and nodded while chuckling under her breath. Before she could respond, she became suddenly quiet, pushing Dan just a little further off the roadway.

Dan heard another car approach. This one seemed to slow down at around the place where he and Beasley left the roadway. The car stopped. He could hear the ticking of the exhaust system as it cooled down.

A door opened then closed. Dan could make out the form of a man holding what seemed to be a cell phone pointed in their direction.

"I know you're in there. Come on out and be quick about it!"

Twenty

Keeping a Beau at Arm's Length

It had been a good lunch. For the better part of an hour, Emily's worries about Dan went away. Her worries returned when she was on the final block of her walk home.

She saw Debbie Wallace swinging back and forth on the swing on the front porch.

"Hey…"

Debbie looked as if she had something weighing heavily on her mind. It was much like the look Emily recalled when she had her first serious conversation with the college student.

"I need your advice," the younger woman started. "I know that you're busy with Dan being out of town and under arrest and all, but I hope that you can give me some advice."

"Other than have three healthy meals a day and don't bet on horses?" Emily joked, hoping to break the tension Debbie brought with her.

"Actually, it's an affair of the heart," she started. "I met this guy. His name is Paul Prescott. He's a grad student; a political science major who looks as if he came out of a catalogue."

"Good looking, I take it?" Emily asked.

"Almost too good," she responded. "I find myself the object of envy whenever he takes me out."

"Does he treat you well, and do you see him as the father of your children?"

"Yes, and I don't know," Debbie sighed. "And there's my problem. He's coming here tomorrow to see me."

"Do you have an idea of why he's coming here?" Emily asked.

"He's coming here to ask me to marry him."

Debbie Wallace just blurted it out.

"I want him to marry me. I want to be married to him," she continued; she then paused.

"I think."

"You sound as if there is some hesitation on your part," Emily commented. "If there is hesitation, you really don't know."

Debbie nodded her head.

"Is part of it because of your miscarriage?"

"He tells me that I'm his dream come true, yet, he's also said that I'm that dream because of my innocence." Debbie gave a quick "Humppf!"

"He doesn't know about you and Hank, does he?" Emily guessed.

"No," she said, shaking her head. "I… haven't told him. I don't know whether I want him to find out. I mean, what if he comes here and finds out from someone else. What then?"

"It would be best if you told him yourself, Debbie. Relationships are built on trust. If you want him to trust you, you need to let him know about your miscarriage and the circumstances behind it. At some point, it will come out. The sooner the better," Emily advised.

"But he might reject me," she pointed out.

"Would that rejection be better now, or do you want to wait a couple of years into your marriage, or after you have children? Do you even want children?"

Debbie pouted for a moment.

"Were you pure before you met Pastor Dan?" she asked.

"I'd be lying if I told you that I had not experienced a man before I met my husband," Emily confessed. "I also told Dan about it the evening we met. It made no difference to him. In fact, he told me that he'd slept with at least one woman before he met me. We concluded that we were only human. We had needs and that there was nothing to be embarrassed about."

"I thought that you... the pastor's wife... I mean..." the younger woman stammered.

Emily gave a soft chuckle then gave Debbie a hug.

"Hard to believe, isn't it?" she smiled. "It's like coming to the realization that your parents had to have had sex at some time to have you."

"Well, my situation was a little bit different if you recall. Hank took advantage of me in a moment of weakness," Debbie pointed out.

"And you haven't been with a man since, I suppose."

"No."

She paused for a moment before she continued.

"And I'm not sure if I want to. Even with Paul."

"Have you talked with him about how you feel?" Emily asked.

"Well, not in so many words..."

"You need to sit down and have a very long and meaningful conversation with this young man," Emily advised again. "If he's coming to propose marriage and you have baggage – whether it's your miscarriage or your doubts about your sexuality, you need to discuss things with him before either one of you makes a mistake you might regret."

Debbie nodded her head slowly. She understood what her mentor told her.

"You may also want to talk with Hank," Emily suggested. "I get the feeling that you still have issues with him."

"Not really, I mean, we talk on the phone on a regular basis," Debbie revealed. "Jaybo at the mental health center suggested it – in fact, we've even had long-distance couples' therapy."

Emily was dumbfounded. It took her at least fifteen seconds to react.

"He raped you. He fathered your child…"

"And I have forgiven him," Debbie interrupted. "When you forgive someone who has hurt you, you take away their power. You should know that."

Emily closed her eyes, took a deep breath, then told her protégé she was right.

"Hank and I are on an equal footing, now, you see?" Debbie pointed out. "There's still some scarring – that's why the therapy – but we've been working things out. Hank's really a good person now that I've gotten to know him."

"Could part of your anxiety about Paul be because of Hank?" Emily probed.

It was Debbie's turn to be dumbfounded.

"Are you saying that you think that I might be falling in love with Hank?" she finally sputtered.

"It's not exactly that, Debbie. You may have forgiven Hank and both of you might be well on the way to putting what happened behind you, but sometime, you'll have to let Paul in on that part of your life. And from what you're telling me, the sooner the better."

"I see," Debbie sighed. "What do I tell him, and when?"

"You told me earlier that Paul's coming to town sometime tomorrow, right?"

"Yes."

"Is he driving or is he taking the bus?" Emily asked.

"He's taking the bus. He's on an internship at the statehouse this summer and he has the day off. I told him to meet me here. Is that alright?"

"I have a better idea," Emily responded. "Meet him at the bus stop and take him into Zeke's for lunch. I understand that the bus usually stops southbound at around one-thirty. I could arrange to have some people there to be standing by in case you need someone to fall back on."

"You'll keep out of sight unless I need you?" Debbie asked.

"You'll know we're there. Unless your boyfriend somehow knows who's who in this town, he'll have no idea who we are or what we're up to."
*****

After Debbie left, Emily called Hank Windom at the lumber yard. It took nearly five minutes for someone to locate the man and get him to the telephone.

"Debbie Wallace was just here, Hank," Emily began. "Your name came up and I wanted to know just what your relationship with her these days is?"

She thought that his hesitation in answering her was the result of his being anxious or shy about the answer.

"We're okay," he finally told her. "We're at peace with what happened and that's that."

"Why do you ask?" he added after a slight hesitation.

"And that's all?" Emily probed.

"Yeah… ummm… what did she tell you?"

"She came here because of some fellow who she believes will be here tomorrow to ask her to marry him. Your name came up."

Emily could swear that she could hear him swallow hard before he answered.

"She's been staying with me and dad the past few days," Hank revealed. "We talked, that's all. She said something about this fellow, Paul, who she's been seeing."

Hank's voice dropped as if he were making a side comment. "If you ask me, I don't think she's sold on the guy. Jaybo seems to think the same thing."

Emily smiled. "Are you and Debbie talking things out with Jaybo Hatfield these days?"

"Yes, ma'am. It was your husband's idea," he continued. "He got Debbie to forgive me about three years ago – about the time she left to go to that school in Tennessee. I thought you knew."

"He doesn't tell me everything," Emily told him. "I did know that she forgave you. I didn't know that you and Debbie were talking things through with Jaybo. Some conversations are confidential. Conversations you have with Jaybo, for instance – or with a pastor, or a lawyer. You can even talk to me in confidence. With Dan being gone, I'm the go-to person in our church. I may not hold the title, but I take my charge just as seriously."

"I have a calling. Someday I'm going to be a pastor in my own right," she concluded, but only in her mind. Her talk with Debbie and her current conversation with Hank revealed that conclusion hidden in the back of her mind. She'd been a teacher, she was trained as a counselor, and since the move to Magnolia, she had the feeling that there was, perhaps, a higher calling she should answer.

"I don't think Paul's right for her," Hank stated flat-out. "And I don't think she wants to say yes, at least to him. At least now."

"I got that impression, too, when I spoke with her," Emily agreed. "Would you be willing to do something to help her tomorrow?"

"What do you have in mind?" he asked.

Emily came up with a plan at the spur of the moment. Hank enthusiastically agreed to take part. They finished their conversation. After thinking things over for a few moments, Emily made a couple of other phone calls to plan for Paul Prescott's visit the next day.

Twenty-One

Just One Step Ahead of the Sheriff

Dan's heart started beating again when he realized that the voice commanding them to come out of hiding belonged to James Hamner.

"Are you two alright?" he asked as they emerged from the underbrush.

"I think you might have scared him out of a year's growth," Beasley smiled, pointing at Dan.

"I take it you didn't tell him about the chip in your backpack," James said. "Well, we're good for an hour or so at least. The sheriff has his men looking for you over near Blackwater Falls."

"Do we get to go back?" Dan queried.

"Not quite yet," James told him. "I have some fresh supplies and a camp set up at Red Creek. You'll be sharing a camper with a couple of agents who'll act as cover when the sheriff heads this way again. When they break camp, you'll hike over to the western trail head of the Blackbird Knob Trail. I believe I can have you cleared by the time we pick you up the day after tomorrow."

"Why can't we just stay at the campground during the next few days?" Dan asked.

"Because the sheriff suspects that there's something fishy going on. He's checked out the campground half a dozen times so far today and will most likely continue to watch until our agents pack up and get out of here in the morning."

"So, I suppose that means that I'll have you for another forty-eight hours or so, eh, preacher?"

Beasley gave Dan a wink. James pretended not to notice while urging the pair to get a move on.

"By the way, I talked with your wife this morning," James told Dan while he was helping load gear into the back of his SUV. "She says not to worry. She was thinking of coming out here herself, but we told her not to. The sheriff might see fit to take her hostage."

"That's ridiculous," Dan sneered. "Why would a sheriff do such a thing?"

"To get a hold of you, that's why. He's dead set on proving that you're the firebug we've been looking for, so he can get hired on as an agent for the Bureau."

"He's been trying to get a job with the bureau ever since he was first elected sheriff," Beasley added. "James and I are starting to think that the perpetrator, at least in this case, has a personal tie-in with the sheriff. Pinkerman might be looking for someone convenient on which to pin the blame."

"Our larger investigation, the one involving the series of similar church burnings, involves a drifter who's been seen in the general area of each of the burnings," James resumed. "Beasley's drawing of the person you described has been shown to a number of our field agents and several dozen witnesses and, well, both of you seemed to nail it. Going through military records, we've identified the suspect as Charles Peter Clark. He was an Army demolitions expert in Afghanistan."

Agent Hamner closed the back end of the vehicle.

"We need to get on down the road and get you dropped off," he told the pastor. "The agents at the campground will fill you in on Mr. Clark."

He urged Dan and Beasley to get in for the short drive to the campground. They arrived to find three small recreational vehicles parked close to each other. Greeting them were a couple resembling Dan and Beasley in as far as their general appearance. They were introduced as Gary Platt and Pam Walker. After introductions were made and gear unloaded, Agent Hamner left to continue his part of the investigation. The foursome settled down to get to know each other over lunch.

Agent Platt had come up from a field office in Tennessee. Like Dan, he played football while he was in high school. His wife, like Emily, was at one time a teacher. They were expecting their second child.

Pam Walker worked out of Erie, Pennsylvania where she lived with her mother and a small menagerie of animals. She had been recently divorced and was quite happy to be out in the wilderness, away from her ex.

After exchanging background stories, the couples collaborated on preparing Dan and Beasley for their hike the following morning. They started by making sure that Dan and Beasley were wearing the same outfits as Gary and Pam. Less than five minutes after coordinating outfits, Agent Platt and Beasley went out to the road and were spotted by Deputy Rusty Collier. He slowed and stopped, giving the couple a once-over.

"Where's your friend, Beasley?" the deputy asked.

"The name's not Beasley," Gary came back as quickly as he could. "I told you earlier my name is Gary Platt. P-L-A-T-T!"

"I was addressing the woman," Deputy Collier shot back. "I'd like to see some identification if you don't mind."

"It hasn't changed since this morning," Beasley told the deputy. "I didn't think I'd need ID just to go for a little walk!"

The deputy insisted on accompanying them back to the camp site to retrieve IDs. Thankfully, when they arrived, Dan and Agent Walker were nowhere to be seen. Beasley went into the camper, hoping to find something to satisfy the deputy's curiosity. Luckily, she found a pair of IDs on a counter next to the kitchenette.

"I still say that you two are the spittin' image of a couple we're looking for," Deputy Collier finally conceded.

He accompanied the pair back to the trail head before heading back toward the north end of the Sods. They waited ten minutes before sticking their heads back out on the road and beating a hasty retreat to the camper where Dan and Agent Walker were waiting for them.

"I think I've been made," Beasley declared when they returned. "Bets that the sheriff and the state police will be up here inside of the hour, giving this place a thorough going over. Stevens and I need to get out of here."

Both couples worked at a feverish pace to get packed and out of camp before the law arrived. When they left, they did some bushwhacking to get to the trail without having to resort to going back out on the main road. It was surmised that Deputy Collier at least would be watching the road after notifying his superiors.

For the second time that day, Dan donned a backpack and ended up following Beasley to the trail. They took a brief break to cover their tracks before continuing their journey to another trail head at the top of the Canaan Valley. The four of them hiked another hour then parted company.

"We're headed back to the trailer," Agent Platt explained. "The deputy we saw earlier assumed that we were on a day hike. If they're sending people out to question us, then it will just look as if we are coming back."

Agents Platt and Walker left Dan and Beasley alone. They walked on for another half an hour before stopping again.

"It probably won't hurt to change clothes before we go any further," Beasley told the pastor. "If there's an air search, our shirts would literally shout out our position and intent."

The move made sense to Dan. The pair changed into khaki shirts, putting the loud plaids they had been wearing into their backpacks before moving on.

They continued at a fair pace, arriving at a primitive campsite where they would be spending the night. Beasley had Dan put up the small tent they were toting – a task he accomplished with supervision and instruction from her.

"You've never done this, had you?" Beasley queried once the tent and the camp had been set. "I would think that someone your age would have at least had a family camping trip or two under your belt by now."

"My idea of roughing it would be to stay at a cheap motel instead of something like a Holiday Inn," he replied. "The ground is hard, the noises are… a challenge and what happens if it rains like it looks like it might?"

"If it rains, you get wet and you're less likely to get a hot meal," Beasley told him. "In some instances, you can scoop out dirt to better conform to your sleeping position. Says so in the Boy Scout handbook. I don't suppose you've ever been a Boy Scout, have you?"

Dan shook his head. "Dad tried to get me interested, but at that point in my life, I preferred playing football."

Beasley just shook her head.

"Surely, your wife would have gone camping, right?"

"No, not that I know of."

"Well, when we're finished with this trek, I might just invite myself over to your place and teach you both," she snorted.

Dan wondered how Emily would react to going camping, especially with the kids. He expressed concern about the lack of privacy and a lack of facilities.

"What we're doing is primitive camping. Unless your family is extremely close, I wouldn't suggest it," Beasley expanded. "There are plenty of public campgrounds out there where you can pitch a large tent and be close to bathrooms. Not pit toilets, but real bathrooms with flush toilets and showers."

Just after eating a light supper, a summer shower slipped into camp. Dan and Beasley hustled to put their backpacks under cover before getting under cover themselves. Dan was soaked to the bone; his clothes clung to him, making him cold.

Beasley stripped off what she wore with little concern about the pastor sharing her tent. After laying her clothes out to dry, she fished around in her back pack and produced a small bar of soap which she took out into the rain.

Dan turned the other way. He wasn't interested in watching Beasley taking her impromptu shower.

"You're an idiot if you don't come out here and take advantage of what nature provided," Beasley called in after less than a minute. "I would at appreciate it if you were to clean up, even just a bit. Body odors are worse in close quarters."

He reluctantly decided that she was right. His clothes came off and he joined his guide. Dan turned to either hide his body or to avoid seeing hers. She handed him her soap, so he could clean off the effects of a day's worth of hiking.

When he finished, he turned to see that she was still there, naked and unashamed, watching him. He was surprised that her appearance did not arouse him. What did strike him was her vulnerability. Dan had every advantage over the woman standing in front of him; he was taller, heavier and presumably stronger than she was.

She on the other hand knew where she was and knew where they were going. Without her, he would be lost – likely prey to whatever lurked out there in this West Virginia wilderness.

In a larger sense, they were equally vulnerable.

Clouds parted; the rain stopped. Rays from the westering sun illuminated them, as if to make a point.

"We are but mere specks, vulnerable to the world around us, as the world around us is small and vulnerable to the rest of the universe."

Dan started to mouth his thoughts.

"We are huge in relation to the seeds of life within us," he continued. "Surely there is a higher power."

"There is a higher power," Beasley spoke out loud. "We know this. How we define the higher power is how we define ourselves."

"Do you know what I'm thinking?" Dan asked.

"No, but I can read your lips and can make a pretty good guess," she smiled. "We should bring our wet things out and let them dry in what little sunlight we have left today."

They hurriedly carried out her suggestion. They waited in the tent until the last vestiges of light were about to disappear before gathering their clothes and packing them back into their packs.

Beasley went on into the tent as she had on the previous night while Dan decided to stay outside to watch the spectacle of stars appearing once the clouds disappeared. He stood in awe of the heavens, this time working out his place in the cosmos; figuring out his place in the mind of God.

Voices interrupted his meditation. Two of them, somewhat loud – flashlights sweeping the ground in front of them as they drew nearer.

"Beasley. Someone's coming," Dan hissed into the tent.

She was up and out of her sleeping bag in an instant. After a quick review of the situation, she had Dan grab their shoes and the backpacks then pulled Dan along to a vantage point just beyond the boundary of the campsite.

The sweeping lights barely missed illuminating the campers.

"Well lookee here!" one of the voices exclaimed. "Looks like someone's out campin'!"

"Quiet!" the other voice demanded.

Dan's grip on Beasley tightened. A brief flash from one of the lights revealed the man suspected of the arson blamed on the young pastor.

The voice demanding quiet, belonged to Tucker County Sheriff Pinkerman.

Twenty-Two

Too Busy to Worry

Emily managed to take a short nap between taking Chloe to the clinic and getting ready to go to Wednesday evening services. Since Steve Mulligan would be preparing the sermon, she had little else to do other than put on a proper outfit and a smile to hide her anxiety.

Agent Hamner called to fill her in on Dan's status. After Dan and Agent Beasley emerged from their overnight hiding spot, they had a couple of close encounters with the county sheriff. Hamner reported that the pair had been resupplied and were headed back out into the wilderness for at least a couple of days while the FBI continued their search for a shadowy suspect.

A few minutes later, Agent Kovalo called to repeat the information she had just received from the agent in West Virginia. Kovalo's call became partly personal after he'd repeated the same information. He revealed that after his family left Pomeroy, they bounced around for quite a bit before settling in western Michigan. After high school, he attended Northwestern in Chicago then from there he joined the FBI. He married a woman he met while attending firearms training sessions, divorcing her only recently.

"What would have happened with us if our family stayed?" he asked Emily.

"Probably nothing," she replied.

"Look, I understand that you might be lonely because of your divorce," Emily continued. "The fact of the matter is that I'm married, now. I have four children and a husband I love and trust, even to the point where I have no problem with him out in the wilderness with another, younger woman.

"I have no idea who assigned you to this case, but I would like to make it perfectly clear that I have no intention of straying from the man I love… not even for someone I lured into kissing me when we were both kids."

There was hesitation on the other end of the line.

"I understand," he said softly. "The truth is that I requested to be on this case because of you. If I've made you feel uncomfortable, I'll withdraw. It's just that I thought it would be nice to reconnect with a childhood friend."

"You're probably good at your job, Eric," Emily replied. "I'd like it if you'd keep on the case, but keep it professional, will you?"

"Yes, ma'am," he told her. "I'll do my best.

"Oh, and thanks for listening," he added.

*****

The Wednesday praise service was shorter than usual. Steve Mulligan's sermon lasted less than two minutes. He meant well, but his endeavor wound up being far short of what he hoped for. He apologized profusely after the service while the congregation was leaving to go home.

Emily's father had a word or two after the service to fill her in on the details of their upcoming trip to Kelly's Island.

"We'll leave early tomorrow morning from your house," her father told her. "Your mother's there right now helping the kids get packed. They're all excited about going."

Lizzie Elston was standing nearby during Emily's conversation with her father. She approached just as Ken Griswold left.

"I was hoping that maybe we could take our trip to the cabin tomorrow," Lizzie stated with a hint of disappointment in her voice. "I understand that you and the Wallace girl have something planned tomorrow afternoon."

"Something came up. I'm sorry, but we're clear to go on Friday," Emily offered. "I'd rather go in the morning, anyway. It's usually a lot cooler."

"I understand," Lizzie smiled. "I believe I'd rather go in the morning myself… say sometime after eight?"

"I'll pick you up at eight-fifteen. It should put us there at a quarter till ten at the latest."

Lizzie agreed to the timing. After she left, Emily went inside to supervise the clean-up of the worship space before locking up and heading for home.

Pandemonium was the word for events at the parsonage when Emily arrived. The boys were upstairs and downstairs at top speeds while Gracie and Hope were meticulously picking out what they were going to take with them on their trip. Emily's mother hovered about, trying to supervise as best as she could.

Gracie and Hope stopped their packing (each had a new suitcase, a gift from their grandparents) when their mother entered the room. After showing off what they planned to bring, Emily helped them pack and organize before getting them ready for bed. Once they settled, Peter and Jacob were starting to argue. It wasn't a loud argument as it was persistent. Emily stepped in as an intermediary. She told Peter to finish his packing then took Jacob downstairs into Dan's study to cool off a little.

"What are you two really arguing about?" Emily asked her eldest son.

Jacob hemmed and hawed for a short bit. "I don't want to go with Grandma and the others," he stated. "Peter says I have to go if for nothing else but to keep him company."

"Is that all?" she asked.

"He was threatening to tell you about... well, about what happened the other day when I came back from not going skinny dipping."

"I take it he thinks that I don't know," Emily smiled.

"I told him that I told you, but he doesn't believe it."

"A long time ago, I heard that there was a TV host who always said, "You can fool some of the people all of the time, or you can fool all of the people some of the time... but you can't fool Mom!""

"Really?"

"I have it from a pretty good source... your grandfather."

"He's pretty cool about some things, isn't he?" Jacob remarked.

"He's plenty smart, too," Emily confessed. "He's one of those people who, after something happens, will take a step back and gently remind you that he knew about whatever happened all the time."

"Did he know that you and dad would, you know, get married just after you met?" Jacob asked.

"Your father and I took him by surprise on that one," Emily grinned. "He set up the date figuring that we'd at least get along. He had no idea that we would fall in love and get married as quickly as we did."

"Did Grandma know?"

"I fooled her, too – but it was the only time I really did. She knew about Eric Kovalo and all the other boys…"

"Kovalo… he was the guy who was here this evening less than five minutes before you got home," Jacob interrupted. "He was the guy at the Father Linguini's the other day – the guy you and Grandma were making a fuss about!"

"Yes, that was Eric Kovalo. The same Eric Kovalo."

"So, he was an old boyfriend? Does Dad know about him?"

"Your father knows about him. He was nothing more than a crush I had when I was a little younger than your brother. I tricked him into giving me a kiss when he came over to the house one time. And that's all," Emily quickly added.

"Like Jaclyn tried to trick me, right?"

"Like that, but it was just an innocent kiss and I did it in front of my parents."

Jacob began to laugh. Soon, Emily joined him. Peter came down just a few minutes later to hear his mother and his brother still laughing, so, he joined in, not knowing why.

There were a few quick and friendly words before Jacob agreed that that a trip to Kelly's Island wouldn't be such a bad idea after all. He winked at his brother then excused himself to go upstairs to bed. Emily knew that the boys would be talking about her first kiss on their way to a shortened summer nap.

It was after midnight when Emily finally went to sleep herself… her dreams punctuated by a feeling that she was being hunted – naked and afraid.

Twenty-Three

Caught

Dan watched in horror as Sheriff Pinkerman and his companion peered into the now empty tent.

"Something looks funny here," the sheriff said, coming away from the tent.

"Think it might be that pastor and the fed?" the other asked.

"Looks like they might have been here," the sheriff speculated. "On the other hand, I wouldn't put it past that damn nigger from the FBI to pull wool over my eyes just to spite me."

The men examined the site as best as they could with just their flashlights.

"Looks like they're gone now, Dad…"

"Maybe they were never here," the sheriff stated. "Or, maybe they're watching us right now."

Both men swept the area around the campsite with their flashlights, barely missing Dan and Beasley several times.

"Most likely a decoy," Sheriff Pinkerman concluded. "We'll need to post someone at each trail head come the morning, presuming that they're still out here. It's late. Let's go back."

The sheriff and his companion left the same way they came, sweeping the beams from their flashlights in front of them to assure that they stayed on the trail.

"We need to get out of here," Beasley whispered when it appeared that the coast was clear. "Pinkerman isn't as dumb as he appears to be. My guess is that he'll be back here without the light inside of fifteen minutes to try and catch us off guard."

"I hope we can get a few things before we go, include some clothing" Dan whispered back. "Somehow the prospect of being found naked in the wilderness isn't too appealing. Besides, I'm a little chilly."

Dan and Beasley stole out of their hiding place to return to the tent. They found clothes and a pair of flashlights, deciding to leave everything else just in case the sheriff and his son came back. The pair went away from the camp at least two-hundred yards before stopping to get dressed. They continued their journey in near total darkness for the better part of an hour before they caught sight of a small campfire further up the trail.

"Friend or foe?" Dan asked, breaking the silence they had maintained since leaving their own camp.

"You stay here while I find out," Beasley told him.

She left him alone, returning fifteen minutes later.

"It's a mixed group," she reported. "There are six, as far as I can tell. Good friends out on an overnight hike. They appear to be winding down for the evening."

"Did you approach them?" he asked.

"No, not yet. We need to let them know we're coming."

They pulled out their still idle flashlights, turned them on and then proceeded to approach the camp.

"Thank God we found you!" Beasley exclaimed as she and Dan stepped into the circle of light.

Dan wondered how believable Beasley's story would be when she started telling the campers about being a pair of lost day-hikers. From the aroma of burning cannabis in the area, he surmised that any story she told would be eagerly believed.

He eventually fell asleep by the fireside while listening to Beasley talking with someone calling himself "Dookie".

The sun was a few degrees above the horizon when Beasley interrupted Dan from his slumber.

"Dookie and his friends just left, headed toward our abandoned camp," she told him. "I filled him in on what was going on. They volunteered to pack out the rest of our things to the trail head, but I told them no. It would likely arouse suspicion.

"They left a canteen of water and a bite to eat," Beasley continued. "It's not much, but it will keep us going, at least until we hit one of the other trail heads."

Beasley went about policing the now abandoned campsite while Dan came to grips with his reality this morning. "Some vacation," he thought. "In and out of jail, now here in the middle of nowhere not knowing which way I'm going…"

He watched Beasley as she disappeared, presumably to do her business, wondering if maybe she was his Moses, leading him to a yet to be defined Promised Land.

"I'm beginning to like you," she confessed when she returned. "You're not like some of the other preachers I've met. You're not quite as... preachy."

"How so?"

"Well, for one, you haven't been a dick about my beliefs."

"It costs me nothing to respect you," Dan pointed out. "I may not believe the same things you believe, but it's not my job to try to convince you that everything you know is wrong."

"Didn't your Jesus command you to proselytize?" Beasley challenged.

"Oh yes. But he also commanded his followers to love God and love their neighbors," he came back. "By being an example, by following that commandment, I am also spreading the word."

Beasley slowly nodded in agreement, as if Dan had made a point she hadn't thought of before.

Dan excused himself to take care of his bladder, returning to find Beasley already shouldering her backpack in anticipation of moving down the path away from the campsite.

"We have a long way to get to where we're going today," she explained when he caught up. "With any luck, we'll run into another team of agents with more supplies."

"Aren't there any edibles up here to sustain us?"

"Well sure!" she said, her voice dripping with sarcasm. "We'll just kill us a bear and have a feast! You know, build a fire and invite everyone we know!"

She stopped right in front of him then turned to confront him.

"All we have to work with is half a canteen of water and a bag of cheese puffs. We're alone in the wilderness and presumably on the run from a vindictive sheriff, and whoever he was with last night. We need to get down off this mountain or hope and pray that someone has figured out our plight and are trying to find us."

"Are you saying that we're lost?" Dan asked.

"I still know my way around, thankfully," Beasley informed her companion. "We're far from lost. Sheriff Pinkerman knows this and is hoping to scoop us up somewhere convenient to him. Our hope is that our people get to us and re-supply us before the sheriff decides to move in."

"I take it that the people we were with last night are not connected with the FBI?" Dan asked.

"After you went to sleep, they were worried that you were a Fed and you were going to bust them."

Dan laughed at the idea. "You know that I'd leave well enough alone, right?"

"I told them that you were pretty mellow and that they had nothing to worry about," she assured him. "I told them that I was really the Fed. They must have giggled about that for a good half an hour."

Dan and Beasley continued their hike without much else to say. She would occasionally point out some of the local flora and evidence of the local fauna. They crossed open fields, often in a hurry, looking over their shoulders for signs of pursuit. There were stands of trees where they could slow down, cool off, and let down their guard.

Beasley slowed their pace at one point, deciding to stop and take stock before continuing.

"I was thinking about last night," she said once they found a fallen log to rest upon. "Did you get a good look at the younger man who was out with the sheriff?"

"I didn't get a good look, but I believe that he was the same person who's been dogging my stay here... the same person you drew for me the other day."

"I caught that he called the sheriff, Dad," Beasley mentioned. "I had no idea that he had a son."

"It could be a younger deputy," Dan postulated. "I've worked in a couple of shops where an older worker would be called Dad... all in fun, of course."

"Shops?" she asked.

"I've turned a wrench or two as a mechanic; sometimes for fun, sometimes out of necessity. Not all preachers make tons of money like the boys on television. Some of us have to work for a living."

"I had no idea."

"I'm relatively lucky," Dan continued. "We had a pretty good-sized church; until the fire, that is. I made enough to support a wife and four growing children."

"Did the fire ruin you?"

Dan had to pause for a while to think.

"The community seemed to pull together, almost before the fire was completely out," he finally answered. "We still hold services. We still take up a collection. Insurance is taking care of rebuilding the structure. I guess I'm still pretty damn lucky."

"Damn lucky?"

Beasley gave Dan an evil eye.

"Yeah... damn lucky," he laughed. "Just like I'm damn lucky to be out here in the middle of nowhere these past couple of days with someone who knows the ropes."

"How so?" she asked.

"In those quiet times when we weren't so scared about being caught by the sheriff, I've had some time to think about our place in the universe," Dan began. "We're all very small and insignificant. Even the powerful and the mighty are just as insignificant. There must be a unifying force. Call it God, or Nature, or science... it's all the same."

Beasley turned toward him while he talked. Somehow, the light caught the young woman's face just right. To Dan, she resembled Emily when the two first met and married. His wife's face flashed through his mind. Emily had become different, yet she remained the same to him. This young girl in front of him became a reminder that he wasn't getting any younger.

"Fifteen years," he thought. "If I had fifteen years taken off me, I would be tempted to take this girl for my own."

Jacob sprang to mind.

He missed his eldest son. Fifteen years and he would have missed the joy of the moment when Jacob was born. The boy was a miracle.

So was his brother and his two sisters.

He recalled the summer he moved his family to Magnolia. Dan Stevens cut through several levels of turmoil to enrich the lives of the people he'd touched.

"Why have I lost touch with my faith?"

Dan didn't realize that he said what he said out loud.

"Sometimes you must doubt what you believe in to better appreciate the love which surrounds you, Dan Stevens," Beasley replied.

Beasley shook her head and looked her companion straight into his eyes.

"I remind you of your wife when she was younger," she stated as a matter of fact.

Dan sat dumbfounded while she continued.

"I've heard it more than a couple of times. It doesn't surprise me. The truth is, I am flattered by the attention. It's never bothered me."

She took a deep breath.

"Until now."

She stood up abruptly.

"We need to get to a trail head," she urged. "For the sake of my sanity and the sake of the relationship you have with your wife; we need to get away from this place."

Dan realized that Beasley was right. Clarity of purpose along with a newfound clarity of what he believed in drove Dan to get up to follow Beasley out of the wilderness and back into civilization.

He had been tempted. He passed the test. Now it was time to move on.

For the next two hours, they quickly traversed varied terrain, stopping only for an occasional sip from the canteen loaned to them by the group of people who had offered them refuge the previous night.

They rested again after making steady progress for two and a half hours.

"How much longer," Dan asked.

Beasley held up one hand and pressed a finger on her lips.

After a few moments silence, he heard someone coming up the trail from the other direction.

And there was another someone.

Beasley swung around to see if there was enough cover in the immediate area so that they could hide.

Nothing.

The best way for them to proceed was to stay where they were and hope that the sounds emanated from friendly people.

They didn't have to wait long.

Less than half a minute after Beasley motioned for Dan to be quiet, they were staring up the barrels of a pair of shotguns.

Hope Stevens appeared at her mother's bedside early on Thursday morning, urging her to get up and make breakfast before her grandparents came to pick her up. Emily followed her youngest downstairs and into a whirlwind of activity. Frank the Dog was going back and forth between Grace and Peter, trying to catch a tidbit. Jacob made French toast and managed to find some frozen sausage patties which he'd thawed in the microwave.

"You'd better not be feeding that dog any of that sausage," Emily admonished Pete.

"It's because he's Jewish and can't eat any pork, right?" Gracie spoke up.

"Who told you that?" Emily asked.

"Daddy says it all the time," she defended herself.

"Just like him," she chuckled and nodded.

She almost caught herself asking where Dan was, until she realized that he was still in West Virginia, still on the mountain.

Eventually, everyone had settled down and final preparations were made for the trip they were about to make. Emily's parents arrived just after nine, driving a rented van.

"You could have taken mine," Emily chided them.

"And leave you with nothing but your feet to get around in?" Ken Griswold pointed out.

"But your car…"

"Is in the shop. It won't be ready until tomorrow afternoon at the latest."

Emily kissed her parents goodbye after making sure that all of her children were secure. Her phone was ringing when she finally went back inside.

She dealt with the usual deluge of pastoral calls while doing the dishes. There were visitors, including Mayor Fair with a progress report on the new church and Steve Mulligan with an apology for the previous evening's sermon.

"I'll do better next time," he promised.

She gently suggested having a long talk with Dan or her father before attempting a "next time".

As expected (or rather, arranged), Debbie Wallace appeared on Emily's doorstep just after noon, wearing an attractive summer dress which looked as if it had been ripped from an early seventies Sears catalog.

"Emmaline Windom chose the outfit," Debbie explained when Emily asked. "It's not too revealing, is it?"

She spun around slowly to get approval.

"I like the print," Emily opined. "If anything, though, it might be a little too modest."

"Paul prefers modest," Debbie replied. "That may be part of the reason I'm still apprehensive about this afternoon."

"And it's probably why you have been reluctant to say anything about your miscarriage."

Debbie nodded her head to agree.

"You definitely need to get it out in the open," Emily continued. "Remember what I said yesterday about keeping secrets. You need to take the initiative. His reaction will give you a good indication as to how your relationship will go later."

*****

Paul Prescott sat in seat C-3 on the southbound bus headed to Huntington, West Virginia by way of Portsmouth, Ironton, and Ashland, Kentucky. Magnolia was a request stop, with pickups and drop-offs on Main Street at Zeke's. The young man watched the unfamiliar terrain unfolding in front of him with anticipation of what would happen when the bus came to a stop.

For the dozenth time since leaving the depot in downtown Columbus, he thrust his hand in his pocket to assure that the small box containing the diamond ring hadn't accidentally fallen out. The bus driver watched him in the rear-view mirror and smiled. He knew what was going on in the young man's mind.

*****

Debbie and Emily had a long heart to heart before leaving the house to meet Paul at Zeke's Café.

"I called some friends of yours after our talk yesterday," Emily revealed. "They'll be meeting us inside and will help support any decision you make."

They arrived to find an empty dining room save for the people Emily invited to witness the day's events. Debbie immediately noted her mother and her younger brother, Donny.

"I had no idea what was on your mind until Mrs. Stevens called us yesterday," Mrs. Wallace greeted her daughter. "Are you alright?"

"I'm fine, Mom, really," Debbie declared while giving her mother a hug. "It's just that had this business to attend to and I needed some room. That's why I stayed with the Windoms in their spare bedroom."

She looked over to and acknowledged Hank and Emmaline sitting in a nearby booth. Mrs. Wallace gave her daughter a kiss before Debbie paid attention to Donnie.

Tricia Michaels, Glenn Michaels' wife and co-owner of the café beckoned for Debbie to come and see her.

"I gave the regular staff the rest of the afternoon off," Tricia told Debbie. "I'll be your server. Glenn and Jaybo are at the counter just in case you need them."

Both men waved and nodded. Debbie knew that if there was going to be a scene, she wouldn't have to worry. Her friends were there, and her friends would be there to support her no matter the outcome of her revelation.

Debbie played a little with Donnie until Emily cleared her throat.

"Time," she said.

The clock over the counter read one-thirty.

Debbie Wallace walked outside, crossed the street and waited on the memorial bench for the bus to come.

196

*****

The bus driver pulled off the divided highway and onto Main Street at exactly one-thirty-four. At one-thirty-five his nervous passenger would step off the bus, allowing the other passengers the assurance that their stops on down the line would be on time.

"Looks like your young lady's waiting," the driver declared while he coasted to his stop.

Paul saw her standing there next to the bench through the front windshield. His moment of truth had arrived. He rehearsed exactly what he would do and exactly what he would say. By the time the bus was back on the highway headed south, Debbie Wallace would be his fiancée. He pulled his back pack from the overhead rack and moved to the front of the bus.

"Good luck," the driver told him while he was stepping off onto the curb.

"Thanks," Paul thought. He didn't think he'd need it. He would be proven wrong within five minutes.

*****

Debbie Wallace greeted Paul Prescott by taking his hand, pulling him toward her and giving him a quick kiss on his cheek. She sensed that he was as nervous as she was. They exchanged a few pleasantries while the bus roared off. Paul missed his first opportunity to propose when she suggested that they go into the café across the street to talk and to get a drink.

He followed her into the café, past the owner (had he known it) and a bearded man sitting at the counter. She led him to a table near the center of the dining room. After seating Debbie, he did a quick inventory of the other patrons before sitting down himself.

Aside from the two men at the counter involved in a quiet conversation, he saw another man, about his age, and a woman, probably his mother. Another party consisting of two women and a small child sat two tables away. The women appeared to be slightly interested – the child seemed to watch him intently. A server came to take their order.

"A couple of house-style iced teas and a small salad for me," Debbie ordered. "How about you?" she asked her escort.

"Nothing for me, thanks," he replied. He doubted that he would be able to keep anything down… at least until he completed the business at hand.

The server went to put the order in to the kitchen. Paul and Debbie held hands across the table.

"I know why you're here, Paul," Debbie stated, looking him straight in the eye. "Before we jump off the precipice, you need to know something."

Part of her expected him to say something like "… whatever you have to say, whatever you think I need to know, it doesn't matter."

He said nothing, so she continued.

"Four years ago, I became pregnant."

"Were you raped?"

Paul's response was immediate. A look of concern crossed his face. "No."

Paul's concern turned to confusion at her answer. He looked around the room again and focused on Donnie.

"That's your son, isn't it?" he said, pointing to the child.

"No. That's my little brother. I miscarried."

"Yeah, right," Paul sneered.

Debbie was starting to become concerned about Paul's shift in attitude. He had withdrawn his hands from hers.

"She's telling the truth," Mrs. Wallace stated, standing up in defense of her daughter. "Debbie lost her child."

"What are you saying? Are you saying that she had an abortion, or is that her child and you're covering for her?" Paul's voice was getting louder as he appeared to become belligerent.

"What are you trying to pull?" he continued. "What kind of woman are you, Debbie Wallace?"

"She's a damn better woman than you'll ever deserve," Hank Windom declared as he stood to confront the visitor. "And she's right. We were just a couple of foolish kids when it happened, that's all. We made a mistake. We all make mistakes. Get over it!"

"You raped her and now you're trying to whitewash the affair?" Paul's face was turning red with anger.

"Tell me what exactly happened," he demanded turning his attention back to the woman he had intended to ask to marry him. "Did you or did you not sleep with that man over there? Did you or did you not have a child because you slept with him? Did you have an abortion? Tell me! Tell me!!"

Debbie was in tears. It was over. She shrunk back to Emily to seek solace.

"Do you have any idea how much you've just hurt this woman?" Emily asked, facing up to the young man. Her voice was calm and steady while she spoke. "It took courage for her to tell you what she just told you, just like it took courage for her to persevere and move on after making the mistakes she made. If you came here to ask for her hand because you thought she was perfect, well, she isn't. I'm not either, nor is anyone in this room. If you came here seeking perfection, you've come to the wrong place. If you came here seeking a partner to share your dreams – to face life with you no matter what it throws at you, then you need to apologize and start mending fences. NOW."

When Emily finished, everyone in the room except for Debbie and Donnie stood and applauded.

Paul Prescott's dream of asking Debbie Wallace to be his wife ended in a flurry of humiliation and embarrassment. He had figured on every possible scenario – every possible way for this afternoon to conclude.

He had not figured on the possibility of her revealing something to him which would taint their relationship in such a way that it would become too much of a burden to bear.

Without another word, he stalked out of Zeke's Café muttering curses as he left. Glenn Michaels followed him out the door and offered to drive him back to Columbus. The offer was accepted. It would be quite some time before Debbie Wallace saw Paul Prescott again.

*****

"Thank you, all of you," Debbie told those gathered around her in the dining room shortly after Paul left. "You've saved me from a lifetime of heartache and regret."

Everyone drifted out of the café except for Debbie and Hank. Tricia came out with a couple of to-go cups of the house iced tea.

"I do have to lock up," she told the couple. "Hope you don't mind."

They thanked their host and headed out the front door to sit on the memorial bench across the street.

"We're pretty messed up, aren't we?" Hank asked when they sat down.

"Yep… no doubt," she agreed.

They sat and watched people going about their business on a warm July afternoon.

"I need to get back to the yard," Hank told Debbie. "You need a ride somewhere?"

She hesitated just a moment before accepting his invitation. In that moment, she saw her children and their father sipping an iced tea in front of Zeke's on a summer afternoon.

Twenty-Five

A Suspect Confirmed

"Get up, Beasley," one of the sheriff's deputies demanded. "You too, reverend!"

Dan and Beasley slowly got up, taking care to keep their hands visible to avoid an accidental discharge of buckshot from one of the over-anxious deputies.

"You're both under arrest," the other deputy informed them.

"Should we cuff 'em?" the second deputy asked his partner.

"Garrett, it'll just make it that much more difficult to bring us down to the trail head in one piece," Beasley replied. "Skip the cuffs and just read us our Miranda rights. And if it isn't too much trouble, do you have something to eat or drink? We lost ours when we were hightailing it away from Sheriff Pinkerman and his buddy last night."

The second deputy, Garrett, seemed embarrassed when Beasley addressed him.

"Who was that anyway?" she continued. "Tell me, Poole, did he hire him a new guy? I can't say that I've seen him before."

"What other guy?" the first deputy, Poole, asked. "He staked out the campground all by himself last night. There was no one with him that I know of."

"He was the guy in the picture," Dan volunteered. "I'd seen him several times before last night."

"Sheriff Pinkerman works alone. Always had and always will. Beasley can tell you that, isn't that right, Beasley?"

"He wasn't alone last night, Poole," she shot back. "I saw the guy, too."

While the exchange was going on, Garrett put down his back pack then produced a couple of bottles of water. He gave them to his captives. They eagerly accepted his gifts. Trail mix was produced, too. Within five minutes they continued their trip toward the trail head with Garrett and Poole following closely behind.

"To answer your earlier question, Dan, we should make the nearest trail head in about an hour and a half," Beasley stated.

"You'd best shut up," Poole growled.

Beasley came to a dead stop then wheeled around to confront the deputy.

"You'd best mind your own business, Poole," she shot back. "That goes for you, too, Garrett!"

In the moment Poole's attention was turned to his fellow deputy, Beasley managed to grab Poole's shotgun, then fired it off into the air. On the shot, Garrett dropped his shotgun and backed off.

"Now that I have your attention, gentlemen, I need your radios and your tracking devices," Beasley announced.

Both deputies handed their electronic devices to Dan while Beasley covered them with their own shotguns. She then had Dan tie the deputies together, chained to a tree. When they were settled, Beasley calmly picked up one of the radios to tell the sheriff where to pick up his deputies.

"By the way," she added, "That man you had with you last night is a person of interest to the agency. You'd best see that our people have a talk to vet him before we return to the trail head."

She then turned off the radio and placed it and the tracking devices just out of reach of the deputies. Taking care to leave enough water to keep them hydrated, she and Dan continued their trek.

"Wouldn't you want to go the other way?" Dan asked.

"Why?" Beasley smiled. "It's going to take the sheriff forty-five minutes to an hour to figure out which of his deputies are missing and to organize a posse to rescue them. They have half a dozen trail heads to cover with no idea which one we'll come out."

"If they figure out which trail head Rosencrantz and Guildenstern took to get into the wilderness, wouldn't they cover that trail head first?" Dan wondered.

"Ooh, nice Shakespearian reference, Mr. Stevens!" she chuckled. "My rationale is the same as you had at one time. If you go where they expect you to be, they'll try to outsmart you by going where they think you'll be going."

"Out on the roadway by the drive-in campground where we started in the first place. But how did you know…"

"I had a talk with a friend of yours. Harold Richmond."

Dan let out a hearty chuckle while Beasley continued.

"He told me about the little cat and mouse game you had when you were in high school. He told me a little about you, too – and about your family. I envy Emily."

"Harold told you about me?"

Dan was shocked.

"What else do you know?"

"For one thing, you tend to doubt yourself," Beasley pointed out. "Or maybe, you doubt your abilities."

"And Harold Richmond told you that."

"No, Harold never said a word. It's just an observation."

"You envy Emily."

"Yes," she admitted. "After four kids, you still put her on a pedestal as if she's the most beautiful woman in the world. But at the same time, you respect her for what she's accomplished aside from raising your children."

"How did you know that?" Dan asked.

"I told you. Observation. Well, that and the talk I had with Emily when I proposed this little outing."

Beasley stopped in her tracks and listened for a few moments before continuing.

"From the moment I met you, you were an enigma. There was something about you which I needed to touch. I needed to know you more than just superficially, so, when the opportunity presented itself, I made a few phone calls to find out as much as I could about you in a very short amount of time."

"In just a couple of hours, including a trip to the outfitters?"

Dan was amazed at the time line from his own point of view.

"You were taking one hell of a risk, weren't you?" he continued. "I mean, I could have been the errant priest looking for a young, innocent victim, you know."

"I know, but I knew you weren't," she pointed out. "Your leaving me alone when I was doing my yoga yesterday proved it."

Both travelers let Beasley's words soak in while they continued down the trail.

"Do you feel any closer to your interpretation of God?"

Beasley's inquiry about an hour after leaving the deputies startled Dan. He was asking himself the same question. She merely vocalized what he thought.

"I believe so, yes," he answered. "I just wish that Emily was here to share what I'm feeling."

"Maybe you can bring her up here once we've concluded our business," Beasley suggested.

"I don't know if she has the stamina to hike into one of the campsites, besides, I don't know how she'll handle not having running water."

"She said the same thing about you, and..."

Beasley cut herself short. She listened for a few moments then ushered Dan off the path to a place where they could hide. For the second time that day, there were voices coming up the trail. When they were about thirty yards away, Beasley relaxed a little. When the pair came into view, Beasley whistled and came out of hiding.

"It took you enough time to get up here," she scolded the pair.

"The sheriff and a couple of his deputies were at the trail head."

Dan saw that the woman talking was agent Walker from the campsite on top of the Sods. She was in the company of agent Platt.

"Your buddy Collier was one of the deputies at the trail head," agent Platt informed Beasley. "He was asking all sorts of questions, especially about you, rather, Walker, here. He was convinced that she was you – and he wasn't satisfied until he ran a set of fingerprints in what he called his mobile crime lab."

"Do you know if they're behind you?" Dan asked, fearing for his safety.

"Actually, they're not," Walker assured them. "Another posse found the posse you tied up, up there, and they were headed to intercept you at the north trail head."

"Garrett and Poole sent them off in the wrong direction!" Beasley exclaimed. "See, I told you that they weren't really such bad guys."

Dan just shook his head.

After laughing off the circumstance, the four of them continued to the trail head where they were met by James Hamner and three other agents. Soon they were on their way to a resort in the valley where the FBI had rented a block of rooms as a command post.

"You say you met your mystery man with the sheriff last night."

James started the debriefing with that simple statement.

"I didn't... we didn't meet him as much as we saw the man," Dan corrected the agent. "It was dark, we were hiding, but we, or at least I saw that it was definitely him."

"It was him, alright," Beasley confirmed. "Man, that was spooky. I nailed every detail."

"We were able to get a positive ID on our person of interest," one of the agents with Hamner chimed in. "He's ex-Army. Served in both Afghanistan and Iraq. His name is Charles Peter Clark. Not much is known about him other than he seems to be the child of a single mother who lives in your neck of the woods, pastor."

"Our question is why did he show-up here at the same time you showed up?" Hamner asked.

"I'd be asking why he was with the sheriff last night trying to track down Pastor Stevens," Beasley stated. "From the looks of it, Sheriff Pinkerman may have a personal interest in this case."

Twenty-Six

The House Isn't empty

"I'm holed up in a cabin at a resort in Canaan Valley."

Dan's words in Emily's ears were the sweetest music she'd heard in at least a month.

"I don't know when I'm coming home," he continued. "It would depend on how soon the FBI catches up with their suspect. They believe that he's connected with the sheriff over here."

"Are you okay?" she asked.

"I'm fine. A little dehydrated and overexposed, but I'm okay. How about you and the kids?"

Emily filled Dan in on her parents' trip to Kelly's island with their children, Debbie Wallace's disengagement and the involvement of Agent Kovalo.

"Was that the same Eric Kovalo you said you had kiss you when you were kids?" Dan laughed when she told him.

"One and the same," she replied. "He's fresh off a divorce as I understand it – and maybe just a little jealous of you."

"I just spent a couple of nights sharing a small tent with a hottie… that is, if you want an excuse to hook up with an old boyfriend…"

"Your hottie warned me ahead of time," she laughed. "So… was she good in the sack?"

"Couldn't tell," he told her. "I've been too damn tired these past few days from being on the run. Besides, we have nothing in common. If anything, her presence made me appreciate you more now than ever."

"If I was the jealous type, I'd say something about you giving the right answer!"

Dan and Emily laughed for a few moments before having a more intimate conversation. As Emily recalled later, the conversation was one of the best ones she'd had with anyone, ever.

After his call, Emily called Lizzie Elston to invite herself over to The Blue and the Gray for the evening.

"We can leave a little earlier – after breakfast, of course," Emily rationalized. She knew that on Friday mornings, there would be French Toast made with fresh eggs from Hatfield's chickens.

She arrived at the bed and breakfast in time for dinner. She opted for the salad, knowing that not only the greens would be fresh, but that Thomas Elston had a way with dressing.

After dinner, Emily settled into the parlor with her host. After a few minutes of exchanging pleasantries, Lizzie called Tricia Michaels to come and join the conversation.

"I've been doing some genealogical research for Miss Lizzie," Tricia started. "Her family tree is quite evident. The stories told by her parents, her grandparents and her recollection of her great grandfather all hold water according to records at the county seat. It's the other side where I ran into difficulty."

Tricia looked at Lizzie, tacitly asking for approval of what she was about to reveal to Emily.

"She knows about my marriage," Lizzie assured her.

"Oh, I really should have known," Tricia confessed.

"That's alright. Tell me. What have you found out?"

"Well, there are some glitches in the Clark family tree," Tricia began. "You mentioned that your husband may have had a brother, or rather a half-brother by another woman."

"My late husband kept detailed records as to who was related to who and in what degree," Lizzie affirmed. "I think I know where in the cabin he keeps them. Emily and I are going over there in the morning to bring them back along with several other mementos. I'd like you to come along if you will."

"I'm sorry, I have other commitments," Tricia apologized. "Let's meet here tomorrow night so I can go over the records and see if they'll confirm what I believe I've found out."

"What did you find out?" Emily asked.

"You may not believe this, but there may be a connection with the fire at the church. The half-brother had a woodshed child himself, and that child had another child out of wedlock. I believe that the grandchild," Tricia paused for a moment, "yes, grandchild is ex-military named Charlie Clark."

"Same last name," Lizzie observed.

"What would be the connection with the fire at the church?" Emily asked.

"For one, his specialty when he was in Afghanistan was demolitions. For another, his mother has ties to this area as best as I could tell. Of course, I don't have the full story on Charlie Clark's family. That's what I'll be following up on tomorrow."

"Should we be worried?"

"Chances are probably not," Tricia assured them. "I'd be vigilant just the same, though, if I were you."

The conversation continued for another hour or so before Tricia excused herself to go home. Emily settled into one of the rooms at The Blue and the Grey for a restful night's sleep.

*****

Breakfast was to die for. Emily excused herself from the table before a second round was offered. She didn't refuse a second cup of coffee, though.

Lizzie and Emily were on their way at just after seven-thirty. Traffic was light on the main roads, at least as far as Peebles. It was eight-forty-five when Emily turned off the secondary road into a driveway diving into a small, wooded area.

"In about two hundred feet, there's a cut out. Pull in far enough so the car can't be seen," Lizzie told her driver.

"Why?" Emily inquired.

"It looks as if someone has been down the drive in the past day or so. They may still be on the property."

Emily pulled into the cutout as Lizzie instructed.

"Should we bring our cell phones?" Emily asked when they exited the car.

"It would probably be best if we left them here," Lizzie pointed out. "If we bring them and one of them rings, we might be giving ourselves away."

After they got out of the car, Lizzie led her friend along the side of the main driveway until they were just about at a clearing where the cabin lay. They kept just inside the tree line and watched.

Lizzie pointed out a motorcycle near the cabin's front porch. A man stepped onto the porch while they watched, pulled down his fly and urinated off the side. He didn't pull his manhood back in until they heard a car coming down the drive toward the house.

An older Honda sedan pulled up to the house. A woman, they could not tell who she was, got out of the car and started pointing back up the driveway.

"Your car may have been spotted. Let's go," Lizzie urged.

They decided to wait for a little while longer. Their subjects stayed on the porch. Eventually, Emily and Lizzie determined that the woman in the Honda was Vera Mace!

"The guy's the same one in the drawing from the FBI," Emily told Lizzie.

"Young Charlie Clark?" Lizzie pondered.

Lizzie's question was punctuated by a blast from inside the house while the motorcycle rider and Vera Mace pulled away from the scene and up the driveway. Both vehicles roared past Lizzie and Emily's hiding place while they watched the cabin go up in flames. Another pair of blasts from up the driveway and Emily knew that the family van had been discovered.

"Shit!" Emily swore. They were miles from nowhere without transportation and with little choice but to walk to the nearest neighbor to use a telephone.

A naked man carrying a cell phone took Emily by surprise.

"Hey, Jake!" Lizzie greeted the man. "Am I glad to see you!"

"Well, I was walking next door over to the resort and I heard the blasts," the man explained. "I called the sheriff. He'll have the fire department over here directly. In the meantime, you can walk over to the resort with me and get things sorted out.

"Oh. Jake Waters at your service, ma'am," the man introduced himself to Emily. "You'll pardon my appearance. Miss Lizzie understands."

Emily took the man's appearance in stride, introduced herself and shook his hands.

"You're the preacher's wife," Jake smiled. "Miss Lizzie told us all about you."

Emily looked over at the retired teacher.

"You?"

"Me," Lizzie confirmed with a nod. "I thought you knew."

"No," Emily chuckled. "It's just that…"

"You just didn't expect it, did you?"

"No," Emily confirmed.

"If certain people found out…"

"They won't, at least from me," Emily assured the former teacher.

Approaching sirens announced the arrival of the sheriff and one of the local fire departments. A call was put out for a water tanker; until it arrived, there was nothing the local volunteers could do other than watch the house burn.

"Was that your car just off the driveway, ma'am?" the sheriff asked Emily when he arrived.

Emily affirmed that it was hers.

"The FBI is sending a man over here to investigate. He's offered to give you a ride home when he's finished."

"The agent's name wouldn't happen to be Kovalo, would it?" Emily asked.

"I believe it is, yes," the sheriff nodded his head.

Emily shook her head. "I thought so," she said. "My being here might hinder his investigation."

Jake stepped into the conversation to volunteer to take both Emily and Lizzie back to Magnolia. "I dress up real nice," he assured Emily.

She agreed to the arrangement. Jake disappeared for about twenty minutes, returning fully clothed and driving an Impala.

"I hear you have a first rate cook over to your place in Magnolia," Jake commented once the three of them were in the car and headed home.

"Then for the ride, you'll have to stay for dinner," Lizzie offered.

For much of the ride back, Jake and Lizzie casually traded tidbits of news about people they both knew.

"Am I to understand that you are both regulars at the resort next door to Miss Elston's cabin?"

Emily was perplexed.

"Well, yes, we do," Lizzie assured her. "I thought you knew that, knowing about my marriage and all."

"I had no idea."

"It's not the sort of place where people go and make it public knowledge," Jake interrupted. "I mean, people running around in their birthday suits are generally regarded as perverts or sex criminals. If you're well-known in your community, like Lizzie, here, and word got out that you socialized with other people while in the buff, you might lose your social standing, or worse."

"Jake works for the BCI out of Columbus," Lizzie added. "He'd lose his job if it was known that he was a regular at the resort."

"You weren't at Lizzie's place on business, were you?" Emily asked.

"Oh, no... at least not officially. I've been keeping an eye on the place informally as a favor to Lizzie, ever since Bob died."

He looked in the rear-view mirror to make eye contact with Emily.

"I've been keeping tabs on you, too, Mrs. Stevens," he revealed. "The business with the FBI over in West Virginia has raised a few eyebrows."

"What am I supposed to be guilty of?" Emily demanded.

"Nothing," Jake replied. "You're just a person of interest because of your husband. He's been cleared, by the way, and so are you.

"We've been conducting our own investigation in conjunction with the FBI," Jake continued. "Actually, we picked up from where the fire marshal left off. They said it was arson, we agreed. Their report was passed on to Kovalo and Barada at the FBI field office in Columbus. Kovalo specializes in arson – Barada works Fuller and a few surrounding counties regarding general matters on a regular basis."

"Why wasn't Eric Kovalo involved in the FBI's initial investigation?" Emily asked.

"He had other matters to attend to, having to do with his personal life and an investigation into a series of fires up near Cleveland. Why he's involved here is another matter."

"It's because of me," Emily confirmed. "He had a crush on me back when."

"One of those junior high first kiss sort of things?" Jake asked.

"Something like that. For some reason he doesn't want to let go."

Jake smiled and chuckled.

"If I had a chance at a woman as pretty as you, I'd be inclined to keep you around myself," he told her.

Lizzie nodded her head and smiled.

After a period of silence, Jake and Lizzie talked about what she and Emily had seen just before the cabin exploded.

"You say you know this woman, this Vera Mace who was with the suspect just before the explosion?"

"Yes," Lizzie confirmed. "Speaking for myself, the woman is a royal pain in the ass!"

"I'll second that," Emily chimed in. "I don't know if I would put it in those terms, but she has been an annoyance."

"What do you know about her?" Jake asked.

220

"Not a whole hell of a lot, except that she seems to be screwing her pastor," Lizzie revealed. "Sorry, Emily. It just had to come out."

"I thought that pastor Simmons came here from West... Virgin..." Emily trailed off, suddenly realizing a connection she hadn't thought about before.

"Do you have any idea where this Vera Mace lives?" Jake asked.

"She has a place, a trailer, just up the river from town," Lizzie told him.

"I'll call the agency and have them pay her a visit – that is if she's still there when we get back to your place."

Emily thought that Jake drove just a little faster than he did when he started out. They arrived at the Blue and the Gray just before lunchtime to find Agent Barada waiting for them on the front porch.

"Been to a fire?" the G-man joked once they were out of the car. "The Highland sheriff called us before he headed out himself. We sent Kovalo. Did you get to see him?"

"No," Jake said firmly. "As a matter of fact, Mrs. Stevens had us rush out of the area before Kovalo arrived. I'll explain later."

Jake then told the FBI agent about the connection between Vera Mace and Charlie Clark.

"We probably need to see the woman as soon as possible – and it wouldn't be a bad idea to question that pastor of hers, too," Barada concluded.

Both policemen went inside to arrange to interrogate Vera Mace. Emily sat outside to contemplate her next move. Lizzie went inside, returning with iced tea to share with her friend out on the porch. The mid-day silence was interrupted a few minutes later by what seemed to Emily to be a flurry of activity. Soon, sirens were heard from the direction of the volunteer fire department. Seconds later, Jake and Agent Barada were out the front door moving as quickly as they could to get in Barada's car and on down Main street.

Thomas came out to join them, acting as if nothing was going on.

"Some house out on River Road just exploded," he mentioned.

"Vera Mace," Emily thought.

Twenty-Eight

Flight

Beasley's voice cut through a dream Dan was having about being in a peaceful place – one which did not involve being chased by someone intent on putting him behind bars.

"Our friendly neighborhood sheriff just left Parsons and is on his way here."

"He'll likely have a deputy here, if there's not one here already, to keep an eye on the place to see that we don't escape."

Dan's head was still in the process of clearing.

"We need to get out of here. Now."

She yanked off his covers, exposing him to the still cold air of a morning in the mountains. He was exposed – naked – without protection.

"Here," she said, handing him a pair of trousers. "Put these on while I get you a shirt."

He swung his legs over the side of the bed, hoping that she wouldn't notice, or if she did notice, she wouldn't say anything about his ebbing erection. He barely got the trousers he had been given on when she came through the door again and threw him a shirt.

"Hamner and our doubles are heading down to the checkpoint, now," Beasley informed him while he was pulling the T-shirt over his head. "They'll divert attention long enough for us to get away."

"Where are my shoes?" Dan asked.

"Your shoes and socks are in the car," she told him. "Once we're out of this jurisdiction, we'll stop long enough so that you can get them on."

Beasley shepherded Dan out to an "arrest me red" Mustang convertible, dumping him into the passenger seat before she went around the car to drive it. Before they'd gotten 500 feet, Agent Hamner's voice came crackling on the radio.

"Seems the deputy took the bait," Beasley explained, while picking up speed. "They're headed north on the main highway towards Davis with a pair of deputies in hot pursuit."

"I take it we're headed south, then," Dan postulated.

"Nope," she smiled. "They're expecting to be tricked. The sheriff will have the south road covered anticipating that we'll head in that direction. We're going to go right past the group headed north!"

"In a car that couldn't be more obvious," Dan commented.

"Exactly," Beasley chortled.

Sure enough, when they got to Davis, they saw a grouping of police and government vehicles massed in a parking lot with half a dozen or more people out of their cars, involved in a loud argument. Beasley drove by without missing a beat, continuing north without a word until they crossed over into Maryland.

"Where are we headed?" Dan asked when they passed the intersection of U.S. 50.

"Magnolia. The long way," Beasley responded. "We'll be avoiding the Interstate in West Virginia, except for a short stretch going through

Wheeling to get to Ohio. After we get some breakfast, I'm going to have you drive for a while, so I can catch a nap."

They pulled into a small restaurant in Oakland where they had a quick breakfast before going back out on the road. Dan tried to call Emily to let him know that he was alright, but she didn't answer any of the numbers he tried to call.

"I'll have an agent get a hold of her and let her know," Beasley assured him.

They went over the route that they would take.

"We'll check in with the agency when we get to Uniontown," she told him. "I should get in a good nap between now and then."

Beasley woke up in the passenger seat about three miles out of Uniontown, Pennsylvania. After making a quick call on the cell phone she carried, she instructed Dan to keep driving until they got to "Little Washington".

"We'll get some lunch there before we head on into Ohio. We should be in Magnolia right around dinnertime," she informed Dan. "By the way, thanks for taking the wheel."

"My pleasure," he grinned.

"I thought you might like it. You were hell on wheels in your younger days, as I understand it."

Dan nodded in agreement.

"So how does someone like you go from being a rowdy little bastard into a minister. I don't understand."

"There are times when I don't understand myself," Dan said. "Most everyone in town thinks it has something to do with my talking with Pastor Kellough on a regular basis. Thinking back, he had a way of nudging people in the direction of where they needed to be. While some preachers preach hellfire and brimstone, Pastor Kellough would talk to people about their spirituality."

"There's something I love about you," Beasley pointed out. "You exude love without all of that messy judgement that I've seen from most other preachers I've met in my lifetime. Your buddy in Davis is one of them. Agent Hamner is another."

"James is a preacher?"

"Well, not properly," she amended her statement. "He talks about God and stuff from time to time, again, not in a pushy way."

Dan smiled. He had only a short time to converse with Agent Hamner but found himself wanting to get to know the man a little better.

"I've been following this case for the past several months, now. You know, the one with all the church burnings. Every last one of the preachers involved are just like you. Quiet, unassuming, and approachable. I like to talk with people like you – people who don't shove God and Jesus down my throat."

"Maybe your suspect is someone who'd rather hear fire and brimstone preaching on a Sunday morning," Dan suggested.

"There's definitely a pattern there," Beasley admitted. "Our investigation seems to support that theory, as well as the other."

"You mean about the perpetrator being ex-Army?"

"Yeah. James must have told you."

"Yes, he did," Dan confirmed.

"Then there was what we saw the other night out on Dolly Sods," Beasley reminded him. "If the man with the sheriff is our guy, it might explain why all the subterfuge. I think the sheriff knows a lot more than he's letting on. In fact, I think that the reason he's after you is to cover his own tracks."

"I'm no detective, but I came to that conclusion when I saw the two of them together," Dan stated.

"Look; I'm just an artist who happens to work for a bunch of detectives," Beasley protested. "I don't catch on to certain things as quickly as other people. Give me a break, will you?

"You did say something to James about what happened up on the mountain the other night, right?"

"Well, yeah. I was debriefed shortly after we got back."

"Now, why are we running? Why isn't the sheriff being questioned and perhaps jailed?"

"Part of it has to do with politics," Beasley explained. "Folks in Tucker County love the man. He's not much of a sheriff, but if push comes to shove, people around here would be in revolt if we were to arrest him. What's more, every other county sheriff in West Virginia has his back. And so do the state police."

"Won't we be taking a risk heading back to Ohio by way of Wheeling?"

"Life isn't without risks, pastor, you should know that. Once the sheriff figures out that his deputies were chasing a bait car, he'd figure out that we were either staying put up at Timberline or headed south past the state park. He'd assume he's lost us. I'm like you were back in your day. I know the roads and I've never been caught."

Dan chuckled warmly, knowing darn good and well that she was probably right, remembering some of the times he'd led Harold Richmond on some wild chases.

Little Washington came up much too soon for Dan's liking. It had been a while since he'd driven something other than a mini-van or a sedate sedan. After a fast-food lunch, Dan asked if he could continue the drive.

"Maybe on the other side of Wheeling," Beasley told him. "If there are any cops hiding on the Interstate between Pennsylvania and the river, I know where they'd be hiding. Besides, I can't let you have all the fun."

Dan agreed with her, besides, he thought that a short nap would be advantageous. He woke up an hour and a half later at someplace called Fly. Beasley had stopped and was talking with an Ohio State Highway Patrolman. She was showing her badge and was explaining their situation.

"I suppose that the gentleman with you is who the sheriffs across the river were looking for," the patrolman postulated.

"I suppose you're right," Beasley agreed. "Truth is, he's my problem. You don't need to concern yourself, officer."

"Well, I suppose I could look the other way while you mosey down the road, little lady."

Dan winced. He didn't suppose that Beasley liked what the policeman just called her.

She just smiled, thanked him and went on down the road. Five miles later, she stopped and told Dan that it was his turn to drive the rest of the way.

"Little lady, indeed," she harrumphed. "I have half a mind to go back and give that man what for."

Dan said nothing while she stewed in the passenger seat for the rest of the trip. He was enjoying the drive.

Twenty-Nine

Clues Falling in Place

Dan and Beasley arrived in front of Dan's house shortly after four to find Agent Barada sitting on the porch swing talking on his cell phone.

"Good to see you made it, and pretty much on time, too," Barada greeted them after putting his phone aside. "I was just on the phone with Jim Hamner. It seems the Tucker County sheriff is about to have kittens over your escape."

Beasley laughed then introduced herself to the local agent while Dan went into his house.

"Where's Emily?" he asked when he came back a minute or two later.

"Your wife went with Lizzie Elston over to a cabin Lizzie has over in Highland County," Agent Barada informed the pastor. "They're back at the bed and breakfast waiting for you."

"I suppose we should head over to the Blue and the Gray," Dan told Beasley. "You'll need a place to stay the night before heading back home."

"I've already booked a room for her," Barada told him. "You go on ahead. I need to debrief Beasley and catch her up on some late developments. Take her car. I'll drive her over when we're ready."

Dan drove to the Blue and the Gray to find Emily, Lizzie and Tricia Michaels out on the front porch. The car barely came to a stop when Emily rushed him.

"Thank God, you're safe," she sobbed. "I was worried sick about you."

Several minutes of reassurance later, Dan and Emily walked up to the front porch to greet the others.

"I hear you had a little excitement while you were in West Virginia," Tricia quipped while he approached."

"You have no idea," Dan replied.

"We had some excitement ourselves," Lizzie spoke up. "We've seen the same person you've been seeing in West Virginia."

"When?"

"Today. He was in Zeke's this morning and out at our cabin just a few hours ago – before he blew it up."

"We think Vera Mace was his mother," Emily added. "If she wasn't, she was at least helping him."

"You may want to see what I have laid out in the parlor," Tricia told him.

She ushered everyone into the parlor where she had set up a computer and several books on a card table over by the fireplace. There were several photographs laid out on the table, too. One caught Dan's eye.

"That's the guy," he said softly, picking up an 8x10 photo. "In Zeke's?"

"Yep… In Zeke's"

"When was this taken? Who took it?" He saw the time and date stamp, as well as a notation of the camera location.

"Security cam footage from this morning," Tricia stated. "It was taken at six thirty-seven just as he was leaving. Looks a lot like the drawing the FBI artist had sent over to Emily."

"That's the guy," Dan repeated. "He's the same one I saw in West Virginia. Any idea who he is?" he asked.

"We know who he is all right," she stated.

"We?"

"Well, I started researching a story about the burning churches the morning your friend's church burned down in West Virginia," Tricia began. "I didn't really start to write about the church fires – rather, I was working on some genealogical background for Lizzie and, her friend, Mr. Clark. This fellow came up as a side note."

Dan wondered if Lizzie had told the reporter the same thing Lizzie told him in confidence about Lizzie's secret marriage.

"Clark had a step-brother, you know. His father got mixed up with a woman before he married Clark's mother. Clark's step brother became a father to an illegitimate child, too, with a woman from West Virginia. She raised their son, while he went, cleaned up his act and got elected sheriff..."

"Of Tucker County?" Dan concluded, ending Tricia's sentence.

She nodded her head.

"This," she said, picking up the picture, "is the sheriff's illegitimate son. Charles Peter Clark, better known as Buddy."

"How do you know his name?" Dan asked.

"Army. He served a couple of tours in Iraq and Afghanistan as a demolitions expert."

Dan let the information soak in a few moments.

"A firebug."

"Apparently," Tricia agreed. "At least that's what Barada and that other guy, the new one on the case, Kovolo, seem to think. Barada will be here in a couple of minutes. Kovalo went out to Highland County to investigate the fire at Bob and Lizzie's place out there. Lizzie and Emily watched Buddy set the place on fire, then leave with his mother, Vera Mace."

Mention of the woman's name hit Dan hard. He thought of her as being mostly harmless. Abrasive, yes, but mostly harmless. Now this.

"Are you sure?" Dan asked.

"We're about 90% certain," she told him. "From what I've been able to determine from the Army, Buddy joined the service seven years ago where he was living in a small town in Pennsylvania. He listed his next of kin as his mother, Vera Whistler. She married a man who raised Buddy as his own until the boy was seventeen. Vernon Whistler drove his car over an embankment into a creek. The coroner stated the cause of death as a heart attack.

"Vera went off the deep end for a while and Buddy went into the Army. Vera was taken in by Pastor Simmons. Simmons' wife wasn't paying him attention – Vera was more than willing and the next thing you know, Simmons is run out of town for having an affair with Vera."

"I thought that Pastor Simmons was happily married," Dan stated. "I've met his wife – she seems nice enough."

"Yes, but she's closing in on three-hundred pounds," Tricia pointed out. "I don't know for sure, but I suspect that Penny Simmons stays married to the pastor only for appearance sake."

"Does the agency know?" Dan asked.

"I've filled them in," Tricia told him. "Emmy and Lizzie's first-hand account of the fire in Highland County confirmed my research."

"I take it that Miss Mace is in custody?"

"She's missing," Emily said. "Maybe dead. Her house went up in flames just a few hours ago."

Beasley and Rob Barada arrived just after the revelations had been made. The information was shared again after introductions.

After a quick conference, Dan and Agent Barada decided to go up to see the remains of the house on the river road while Emily, Lizzie and Beasley stayed behind.

"Who are they?" Dan asked Agent Barada as they approached the scene of the fire.

"The man on the left is Jacob Evans. He's with the Ohio Bureau of Criminal Investigation," Barada informed the pastor. "The other fellow is Eric Kovalo. He's one of ours. Both of them are crack arson investigators."

Kovalo directed Barada to a place to park in a yard with the smoldering ruins of a recent fire. When he was introduced to Pastor Dan, he broke into a wide smile.

"You, sir, are the luckiest man in the world," he said, pumping Dan's hand. He explained his connection with Emily.

"I've heard about you," Dan told the agent. "We'll have to have you over for dinner when this is all over."

Sheriff Roy joined the small group almost immediately.

"We found a body," he said. "No identification, yet, but we believe that it's Miss Mace."

"I'm sorry to hear that," Dan declared. "She was a pain in the neck, but if it was her who died here…"

His voice faded away, dissolving in a silent prayer for the deceased.

Dan and the investigation team spent an hour and a half combing through the hot ashes to see if there was any indication of how the fire started. Dan pointed out some of the same patterns he'd seen at the fire in Davis.

"James showed me what to look for when he took me to the fire in Davis," Dan revealed. "I wish he was here. He's a good man."

"You have a sharp eye," Kovalo complimented the pastor. "Have you ever considered changing careers?"

"I've come close these past few days," Dan replied. "Someone showed me that I'm just fine doing what I've been doing."

A few minutes later, Dan noticed a patch of bronze within the wreckage. He bent down to retrieve a pair of plaques missing from the collection at The Community Church. Looking further, he found an unburnt envelope containing a card as well as a pair of plaques he recognized from one of his former churches.

"Lodi," he mumbled. "Why the church at Lodi?"

The answer made itself known too quickly for Dan's liking.

"Lodi must burn!"

The card was hand-written. It was filled with malice in just three words:

"Lodi must burn!"

He pocketed the card and searched some more. He found a dozen other similar envelopes containing similar threats and similar plaques from Honor Rolls like the one destroyed in the fire at Magnolia.

"Found something?"

Agent Bob Barada's voice cut through Dan's concentration concerning the cards and what they might mean.

"Yeah… look here," he said, showing the FBI agent his find. "I wonder if these might tie into the fires James Hamner was telling me about."

238

Barada looked at the envelopes he'd been handed, then summoned the other two investigators.

"We need to take these over to our team in West Virginia and see what they may have to say about this," Kovalo stated.

"Beasley may know something," Dan suggested. "She's back at The Blue and the Gray with Emmy and Miss Lizzie."

"C'mon. Let's go back and find out," Barada said, heading back to his car.

Dan and Barada were back at the bed and breakfast inside of ten minutes. Barada took Beasley aside to show her Dan's find. Dan and Emily made plans to go home to have dinner.

"You could stay," Lizzie Elston suggested.

"We could, but we need some time alone," Emily countered. "We'll come by and catch up in the morning."

"Would you like to use my car?" Beasley offered.

"We can take our van," Dan stated. "By the way, Emmy, where did you park it?"

"It's… blown to bits, courtesy of your local arsonist," Lizzie informed him.

Dan looked over at Emily. She nodded to let him know that Lizzie had told him the truth.

They took advantage of Beasley's offer – driving to Ding's up in Prentiss for an intimate dinner, followed by an early bedtime at their house.

"The situation would certainly resolve itself in the morning," Emily assured her husband while they got settled for the night.

"I guess so," he agreed. "I guess so."

*****

Dan woke up at one-thirty, barely three hours after going to bed.

"Lodi. Why Lodi?"

The question rolled around in his head a few times, keeping him awake.

"Why Lodi?"

He really didn't like his time there. He recalled wanting another job almost as soon as he accepted the job as youth pastor.

"Why Lodi?"

He wandered the empty house while Emily slept.

It seemed as if the only way to cure his restlessness would be a drive. Dan put on some clothes, grabbed his wallet and the keys to Beasley's car, kissed Emily on the forehead, then took off.

Prentiss wasn't too far – Columbus wasn't either. Before he knew it, he was on the Interstate headed north and east. By the time he passed Delaware, he knew that he wouldn't stop until he was in Lodi.

He had to know why... and as much as he loathed working there, he felt as if it was his fate to go there – to keep the place he loathed from meeting the same fate as the church in Davis as well as his church in Magnolia.

Thirty-One

In the Act

Hints of the gathering daybreak crept across the eastern sky when Dan Stevens pulled into the parking lot of his old church at Lodi. Despite being nearly eighteen years since he left to go to Pomeroy, he knew the place like the back of his hand.

Not much had changed. Hopefully, the doors would be unlocked as they always had been, providing refuge to anyone who might have needed it. He started the car back up, so he could park on a side street a block and a half away, thinking that he would be less obvious in his presence to anyone intent on doing harm to the church. Thankfully he had the foresight to wear his running shoes in case he needed a quick getaway.

Other than the protests of a small dog, Dan's progress to a side door went unnoticed. A few twists and turns through various parts of the building eventually led him into the main sanctuary. It was just as he remembered it – the pews arcing around to face the main stage – the approaching dawn back lighting the stained-glass windows looking out to the east.

A brief glimmer of a flashlight caught Dan off guard. He backed off, hoping to hide, but stumbled over a small obstacle behind him. Before he could utter a small curse, a voice commanded him to stay where he was.

"You're at the end of the road, preacher," the voice growled. "You better hope that heaven is real. You're going there or to hell real soon."

A dark form yanked him to his feet.

"The way I have it figured," the voice continued, "you'll be there inside of ten minutes, tops."

"Well, I see I finally have my man!" Sheriff Pinkerman's voice chimed in. "You're a pretty fair piece away from where I last saw your sorry ass, pastor Stevens."

Dan said nothing. Nothing would change. He was caught in a trap with little hope of escape.

The sheriff grabbed Dan's shirt then shoved him along out of the sanctuary and into what Dan remembered as the music room. Pinkerman shone a light directly into his face.

"I want you to have a good look at me, boy. I'm going to be the last person you'll ever see. Have a real good look."

Dan saw malice; but he also saw a glimmer of fear.

There was a "snap" on the other side of the now-closed door.

"Gotcha both," the other voice said. "Both of you gonna die, just like I did in my dear, old mother."

Sheriff Pinkerman's face paled. He dropped his flashlight and ran to the door, pounding on it and pleading to be let out. After about a minute, he slumped down, his back to the door. He sobbed uncontrollably. Dan went to console his former nemesis.

"There's another way out," he told the lawman. "If it's still here, I know a way into the undercroft."

Dan stamped on the floor for half a minute before finding what he wanted under a rug in the middle of the room. Tearing away the rug, he uncovered a trap door. He took the sheriff's flashlight and illuminated the darkness underneath.

"Looks like the ladder's still here," Dan observed. "Let's get out of here before that crazy son of yours decides to blow the place up with us in it!"

"It's no use," the sheriff sighed.

Before Dan could react, Sheriff Pinkerman pulled his pistol from its holster, placed the muzzle under his chin and pulled the trigger.

=Click=

Not the explosion Dan expected, along with the spectacle of blood and brains decorating the wall behind the other man's head.

=Click=

A second try yielded the same result.

=Click=

As did a third.

The sheriff slumped over, defeated.

Apparently, the son took no chances at his revenge, emptying the sheriff's pistol on the sly.

Dan attempted to encourage the sheriff to leave the room by way of the trap door, but to no avail. He pleaded, hoping to escape before hearing the explosion which would mark their doom.

"Save yourself, pastor," the sheriff told him. "My life ain't worth jack-shit now, anyway. If I live, I'm headed to jail. Don't you see, pastor? Don't you see?"

While the sheriff was wallowing in self-pity, Dan heard sirens approaching and noticed that there was some sort of hubbub in the outer hall. A light appeared from the trap door leading to the undercroft. A familiar head popped up and started to scold him.

"What made you think you could sneak off with my car and get away with it, Stevens?" It was Beasley.

"BOYS, THEY'RE IN HERE!" she shouted, coming to Dan's side.

In seconds, the door to the music room was forced open. Several agents, including Barada, Kovalo and Hamner swarmed in to confront the sheriff and pull Dan to safety.

"You okay, Dan?" James Hamner asked.

"I suppose, so… but how? What? I'm confused. I prayed for a miracle – now this…"

Agent Hamner laughed. "Let's just say that we keep our feathers numbered for just such an occasion! We have a few loose ends to tie up. We'll debrief you later. Now, you need to go with Beasley to recover her car."

Dan and Beasley left the building, past a group of uniformed officers in the process of searching and cuffing the same man Dan had seen several times previously.

"I prayed that you would make it out safely," Beasley remarked while they strolled up to her car. "I don't really understand this Jesus thing, but I do know that positive thoughts directed to someone you care for can help sometimes."

She let her remark soak in for a moment before adding: "Of course, having a tracking device on the car helps a lot, too."

Dan's mouth flew open. "You followed me?"

"Technically, it was Barada and Kovalo. I was just along for the ride!"

Beasley kissed Dan on the cheek before going to the passenger side of the car. "We need to take you to the field office in Akron before I take you home," she told him when she got in. "There will be a debriefing before we release you. With any luck, you can be home by four this afternoon."

He drove where she instructed him to drive. The field office was on the second floor of what appeared to Dan to be just another office building of glass and steel. There were three hours of questioning by several different agents covering various aspects of what he had seen and heard in the past week.

His last session was with James Hamner.

"I want to thank you for doing what you did," the agent started. "That last bit was really stupid of you and could of cost you your life if it hadn't been for Beasley."

"She seems to have been my guardian angel," Dan remarked.

"I thought you were losing your faith to where you didn't believe in angels, pastor."

"Beasley helped me get some of my faith back."

"There's still some missing?" Hamner asked.

"I still have some niggling doubts," Dan admitted. "Most of it has to do with the rules imposed by others of my faith. I may have to study and perhaps change course."

"God loves you no matter where you are in your faith journey."

Dan wasn't sure who made the statement. It didn't matter who said it in the long run – it mattered that the statement stuck in his mind in the first place.

The remainder of Dan's session with James Hamner was short and to the point. He was thanked for his assistance in resolving the string of church fires. "Buddy" Clark was arrested before he could initiate a fire at the church in Lodi. On his arrest, he admitted to setting the other fires under investigation as well as the murder of his mother.

A point was made at that meeting that there was a reward being offered for information leading to the arrest of the person responsible for the string of church fires. When he was offered the reward, Dan refused, asking that the reward money be distributed to the various churches affected by the arson.

When they were finished, Agent Hamner walked Dan out of the interrogation room and into the reception area.

Emily, Lizzie Elston and Beasley were waiting for him. Emily scolded her husband for running off in the middle of the night without leaving word. Arrangements were made for Dan and Emily to drive Beasley's car back to Magnolia. Beasley would ride down with Lizzie then presumably from there, head back to her place in West Virginia.

"She loves you, you know," Emily stated when they were half way between Akron and Magnolia.

"Who?" he asked.

"Beasley, as if you didn't know," Emily informed him.

"She told me while you were talking with the other agents," she added.

Dan sat silent for a few miles to digest what he had just been told.

"You know that nothing went on between us," he finally said in his defense.

"I know that," she smiled. "She loves me the same way. We've made an impression on her which may change her whole life."

Emily stayed quiet for a few miles.

"You and I had the same problem for a while. While you were losing your faith in God. I was losing my faith in you."

"I have it back," Dan stated.

"And my faith in you is back," she responded. "I had a talk with Beasley. She believes that you had an epiphany while you were up on the mountain."

"Yes, I did. I realized where I was in the grand scheme of things – and that God is in charge. I'm good to go back."

"I know," she said. "I know."

Thirty-Two

The Odds and Ends

Dan felt as if he spent every waking moment of the next month giving depositions to the FBI, and the Ohio BCI.

He developed a friendship with Eric Kovalo, to Emily's slight annoyance. The agent confessed to his desire to strike up a romance with the pastor's wife, to Dan's amusement. He managed to turn the tables a bit, managing to get Kovalo's ex-wife to at least talk with him again. She agreed to counseling, too. By Christmas, there was talk about reconciliation.

James Hamner engaged Dan in a series of long talks "off the record" about spiritual matters. He managed to nudge Dan in a slightly different direction than he'd been going. At the end of the talks, Dan felt the need to be somewhere else, or to at least do something different. He promised himself (and Emily) that he would explore some possibilities at some point after the new year.

Beasley stayed for a while with Lizzie Elston at The Blue and the Gray. Emily joined them from time to time, taking her children (well, just Grace and Hope – the boys were soon up to their necks in football) with her. Hope occasionally dropped little hints about her mommy and the new lady drawing faces with each other. On Dan and Emily's anniversary weekend, Beasley attended services and came forward to be baptized.

Rob Barada filled in some of the blank spaces having to do with the various acts of arson committed by Buddy Clark. Buddy was diagnosed with PTSD. His way of dealing with his past was to set fires. There was an element of hatred for his mother involved, as well as hatred for the man he said was his father.

Sheriff Pinkerman voluntarily gave up his post as sheriff. His involvement in at least the attempted arson of the church in Lodi left him open to numerous federal charges – charges which were not filed due to the intervention of FBI agent Hamner.

Rebuilding the Magnolia Community Church went ahead at a great pace, thanks to some unusually good weather lasting into the first week of December. With three weeks left to go before Christmas, construction at Magnolia Community Church looked to be just about done. Due to details which had to be finished and the school board's reluctance to sponsor some of the traditional activities usually held at the church during the pre-Christmas season, most of the traditions were moved to other venues. The board did allow the "Roman marketplace" enactment in the school, but to view the "Living Crèche", one had to go to the church parking lot where the exhibit was set out in front of the steps of the new building.

Most of Magnolia pitched in. Downtown was decked out in colorful lights, as were many of the houses. Glenn Michaels unofficially organized a "tour of lights" for the month of December, terminating at Zeke's Cafe, where visitors from out of town could enjoy a cup or two of hot cocoa before heading back home. The tour ended up being a moderate success, drawing people from as far away as Columbus. They were not disappointed.

Except for a week of rain, weather was particularly mild between Thanksgiving and Christmas. Hope Stevens kept asking about snow – Dan kept pointing out to her that there didn't have to be snow for there to be Christmas. His answer didn't satisfy her, so she kept asking.

On the morning of December 24th, Dan got up a little earlier than usual to head down to Zeke's for breakfast and to say a word or two on the radio about Magnolia Community Church and the season itself. Before he could get out of the house, Hope toddled down the stairs. He spent a few extra minutes to get her dressed to go with him.

There weren't a lot of people at the café, understandable because of the Holiday. Those few people who were in attendance enjoyed Dan's talk and were particularly taken with Dan's youngest daughter.

Dan and Hope strolled out into a cold, clear morning, taking the long way home to visit the church. What Dan didn't say to anyone (not even to Emily) was that the construction supervisor and the county building inspector had been through the building the day before, declaring that it was ready for occupation. While they walked toward the building, Dan reached in his pocket to assure himself that he still had the key given to him the day before.

Emily and the other children were waiting at the front door as Dan and Hope arrived. She gave him a scolding look as he walked up.

"I can't get anything past you, can I?" Dan laughed when they mounted the steps to the entrance.

"Daddy called and told me that he talked with the building inspector just after the inspector left the church," Emily confessed. "He and Mom asked for us to wait for them. They're on their way."

Dan inserted the brand-new key into the door then waited for Emily's Parents. They arrived in less than two minutes, along with an assortment of other people who just happened to find out what was going on.

"I thought I was going to keep this quiet," Dan said to those assembled. "Since we seem to have been found out, maybe we can delay for a while longer to call some other folks over."

A quick decision was made, and the official opening of The Magnolia Community Church would be held at noon. There would be a quick prayer service, followed by an open house. Word was relayed to Glenn at Zeke's Café; most of the community was aware of the plan prior to the hastily organized event.

The event seemed to be as quickly organized as the building of the church. When Dan and his family arrived at eleven forty-five, there were chairs set up, a dais and a red and green ribbon set up by the entrance.

There were also a pair of easels set up near the dais with yet to be unveiled artwork waiting to be unveiled.

Speeches were made, congratulations were passed then both easels were uncovered.

A gasp went through the audience when it was revealed that both easels had half of the Honor Wall each. This time, each of the newly restored plaques was accompanied with a laminated drawing of each honoree drawn by the young woman Dan spotted in the crowd just as the walls were being revealed.

Beasley smiled and winked at him, mouthing "I'll explain how later" to the very surprised pastor.

He looked over to Emily. She was smiling like the cat that ate the canary, nodding her head to let him know that she was in on the surprise as well.

The unveiling was followed by the ribbon cutting. After a pair of quick invocations by Dan and Emily, the doors opened, and the people streamed in.

Dan planned to go in with the first wave of people to give them a personal guided tour of the facility. He was waylaid by Steve and Millie Mulligan who had questions about the community Christmas dinner which he already thought he had settled. What he didn't notice during the conversation was that the people going inside were carrying packages and were almost immediately employed in setting up Christmas decorations.

To say the least, Dan was stunned when he finally made it through the front door. His mother-in-law was busily directing the effort to prepare the church for Christmas Eve Services.

"You've always told me that God is love," Emily told him while hanging on his shoulder. "You don't need any more proof that he is alive than watching what's being done here this afternoon, do you?"

He smiled and cried at the same time, bringing his wife closer to him while the people of Magnolia continued their task of making the new building home. What was to be a short celebration lasted well into the cold winter night. Warm hearts didn't seem to mind.

Of course, they never did.

Bruce Harrell is a refugee from southern Ohio, living in Texas with his better half (a self-professed "Crazy Old Redhead"), a Chihuahua he tries to pass off as a Hawaiian dog, a cat named Morticia and Red the Wonder Dog. When he's not writing, Bruce is usually off somewhere shooting pictures of stuff which interests him. He is "retired" from twenty years in sales and another twenty years working in radio to live the life of a struggling author.

The author speaks:

You, the reader, may have noted a couple of loose ends in this story. I thought about adding an epilogue but decided against it. Instead, some of the loose ends will be dealt with in my next book – _Goodbye to All That_.

Hope to be seeing you there!

Made in the USA
Middletown, DE
13 February 2022

61083802R00144